MICHAEL MOORCOCK

Winner of the Nebula and World Fantasy awards
August Derleth Fantasy Award
British Fantasy Award
Guardian Fiction Prize
Prix Utopiales
Bram Stoker Award
John W. Campbell Award
SFWA Grand Master
Member, Science Fiction and Fantasy Hall of Fame

"Moorcock's writing is top-notch."
—*Publishers Weekly*

"Moorcock is a throwback to such outsized 19th-century novelistic talents as Dickens and Tolstoy."
—*Locus*

"No one … is doing more to break down the artificial divisions that have grown up in novel writing—realism, surrealism, science fiction, historical fiction, social satire, the poetic novel—than Michael Moorcock."
—Angus Wilson

"He is the master storyteller of our time."
—Angela Carter, author of *Nights at the Circus*

PM PRESS OUTSPOKEN AUTHORS SERIES

1. *The Left Left Behind*
Terry Bisson

2. *The Lucky Strike*
Kim Stanley Robinson

3. *The Underbelly*
Gary Phillips

4. *Mammoths of the Great Plains*
Eleanor Arnason

5. *Modem Times 2.0*
Michael Moorcock

6. *The Wild Girls*
Ursula Le Guin

MODEM TIMES 2.0

plus...

MODEM TIMES 2.0

plus

"My Londons"

and

"Get the Music Right"
Outspoken Interview

MICHAEL MOORCOCK

PM PRESS | 2011

"My Londons" was originally published in a slightly different form in *The Financial Times* (London), June 26, 2009.

An earlier version of *Modem Times* appeared in the second volume of *The Solaris Book of New Science Fiction*, edited by George Mann. (Solaris, 2008)

Series Editor: Terry Bisson
Assistant Editor: Allan Kausch

ISBN: 978-1-60486-308-6
LCCN: 2010927786

PM Press
P.O. Box 23912
Oakland, CA 94623
PMPress.org

Printed in the USA on recycled paper.

Cover: John Yates/Stealworks.com
Inside design: Josh MacPhee/Justseeds.org

CONTENTS

MODEM TIMES 2.0
A JERRY CORNELIUS STORY

MINIATURE phones you carry in your pocket and that use satellite tracking technology to pinpoint your location to just a few centimeters; itty-bitty tags that supermarkets use to track their products; bus passes that simultaneously monitor your body temperature to find out how often you are having sex . . .

—James Harkin, *New Statesman*, January 15, 2007

Mother Goose: Youth, why despair?
The girl thou shalt obtain
This present shall her guardian's sanction gain
The GOOSE *appears*
Nay doubt not, while she's kindly used, she'll lay
A golden egg on each succeeding day;
You served me—no reply—there lies your way.

—*Harlequin and Mother Goose; or, The Golden Egg* by Thos. Dibdin, 1st perf. Theatre Royal, Covent Garden, Dec. 29, 1806

LIVING OFF THE MARKET

1. A MYSTERY IN MOTLEY

> GALKAYO, Somalia—Beyond clan rivalry and Islamic fervor, an entirely different motive is helping fuel the chaos in Somalia: profit. A whole class of opportunists—from squatter landlords to teenage gunmen for hire to vendors of out-of-date baby formula—have been feeding off the anarchy in Somalia for so long that they refuse to let go.
>
> —*New York Times*, April 25, 2007

> Madness has been the instigator of so much suffering and destruction in the world throughout the ages that it is vitally important to uncover its mechanisms.
>
> —Publisher's advertisement, *Schizophrenia: The Bearded Lady Disease*

THE SMELL OF PINE and blood and sweet mincemeat, cakes and pies and printing ink, a touch of ice in the air, a golden aura from shops and stalls. Apples and oranges; fresh fruit, chipolata sausages. "Come on, girls, get another turkey for a neighbour. Buy a ten-pounder, get another ten-pounder with it. Give me a fiver. Twenty-five pounds—give us a fiver, love. Come on, ladies, buy a pound and I'll throw in another pound with it. *Absolutely free*." Flash business as the hour comes round. No space in the cold room for all that meat. No cold room at all for that fruit and veg. The decorations and fancies have to be gone before the season changes. "Two boxes of crackers, love, look at these fancy paper plates. I'll tell you what, I'll throw in a tablecloth. Give us a quid for the lot. Give us a quid thank you, sir. Thanks, love. That lady there, Alf. Thank you, love. Merry Christmas. Merry Christmas."

"I hate the way they commercialize everything these days."

"That's right, love. A couple of chickens, there you go, love—and I'll tell you what—here's a pound of chipos for nothing. Merry Christmas! Merry Christmas! Merry Christmas! Seven-pound sacks. Two bob. No. Two sacks for half a dollar. Half a dollar for two, love. Last you the rest of the year. Stand up, darling. Here, Bob, hold the fort, I'm dying for a slash. Dolly mixtures, two bags for a shilling. Two for a shilling, love. That's it, darling! Genuine Airfix they are, sir. All the same price. Those little boys are going to wake up laughing when they see what Santa's brought them. Go on, sir, try it out. I'll throw in the batteries. Give it a go, sir. No, it's all right, son. Not your fault. It went off the curb. I saw it happen. Go on, no damage. I'll tell you what, give me ten bob for the two. Tanner each, missis. You'll pay three and six for one in Woolworths. I'll tell you what. Go in and have a look. If I'm wrong I'll give you both of 'em free. Hot doughnuts! Hot doughnuts. Watch out, young lady, that fat's boiling. How many do you want? Don't do that, lad, if you're not buying it. Get some cocoa. Over here, Jack. This lady wants some cocoa, don't you, darling? Brussels. Brussels. Five pounds a shilling. Come on, darling—keep 'em out on the step. You don't need a fridge in this weather."

Now as the sky darkens over the uneven roofs of the road, there's a touch of silver in the air. It's rain at first, then sleet, then snow. It *is* snow. Softly falling snow. They lift their heads, warm under hoods and hats, their faces framed by scarves and turned up collars. (Harlequin goes flitting past, dark blue cloak over chequered suit, heading for the Panto and late, dark footprints left behind before they fill up again.) A new murmur. Snow. It's snow. "Merry Christmas, my love! Merry Christmas." Deep-chested laughter. Sounds like Santa's about. The students stop to watch the snow. The men with their children point up into the drawing night. "Merry Christmas! Merry Christmas!" It's a miracle. Proof that all the disappointments of the past year are disappearing and all the promises are really going to be kept. "Happy Christmas, darling. Happy Christmas!" The Salvation Army stops on the corner of Latimer Road. The tuba player takes out his vacuum of tea, sips, blows an experimental blast. Glowing gold flows from the pub and onto the cracked and littered pavement. A sudden roar before the door closes again. "Merry Christmas!"

A boy of about seven holds his younger sister's hand, laughing at the flakes falling on their upturned faces. His cheeks are bright from cold and warm grease. His thin face frowns in happy concentration.

"Here you go, darling. Shove it in your oven. Of course it'll go. Have it for a quid." All the canny last minute shoppers picking up their bargains, choosing what they can from what's too big or too small or too much, what's left over or can't be sold tomorrow or next week. It has to be sold tonight. "I'll tell you what, love. Give us a monkey for the lot." *Merry Christmas. Merry Christmas*—sparking toys—little windmills, tanks and miniature artillery—glittering foil, tinsel and trinkets. Clattering, clicking, nattering, chattering, clanking, whizzing, hissing, swishing, splashing the street with cascades of tiny lights. Multicoloured bulbs winking and shivering, red, white, blue, green, and silver.

Stacks of tightly bound trees, already shedding ripples of needles, some rootless, freshly sawn, some still with their roots. The smell of fresh sawdust, of earth . . . The smell of a distant forest. The boy knows he has to get a big one and it has to have roots. "Five bob, son. That's bigger than you, that is. Give us four. Six foot if it's an inch. Beautiful roots. What you going to do with it after? Plant it in the garden? That'll grow nicely for next year. Never buy another tree. That'll last you a lifetime, that will."

Jerry holds his money tight in his fist, shoved down between his woollen glove and his hot flesh. He has his list. He knows what his mum has to have. Some brussels. Some potatoes. Parsnips. Onions. Chipolatas. The biggest turkey they'll let him have for two quid. Looks like he'll get a huge one for that. And in his other glove is the tree money. He must buy some more candle-holders if he sees them. And a few decorations if he has anything left over. And some sweets. He knows how to get the bargains. She trusts him, mum does. She knows what Cathy's like. Cathy, his sister, would hold out the money for the first turkey offered, but Jerry goes up to Portwine's to the chuckling ruby-faced giant who fancies his mum. Nothing makes a fat old-fashioned butcher happier than being kind to a kid at Christmas. He looks down over his swollen belly, his bloodied apron. ("Wotcher, young Jerry. What can I do you for?") *Turkeys! Turkeys! Come on love. Best in the market. Go on, have two.* ("Ten bob to you, Jerry.")

There's a row of huge unclaimed turkeys hanging like felons on hooks in the window. Blood red prices slashed. Jerry knows he can come back. Cathy smiles at Mr. Portwine. The little flirt. She's learning. That smile's worth a bird all by itself. Down towards Blenheim Crescent. Dewhurst's doing a good few, too. Down further, on both sides of the road. Plenty of turkeys, chickens, geese, pheasants. "Fowl a-plenty," he says to himself with relish. Down all the way to Oxford Gardens, to the cheap end where already every vegetable is half the price it is at the top. The snow settles on their heads and shoulders, and through the busy, joyful business of the noisy market comes the syncopated clatter of a barrel organ. *God Rest Ye, Merry Gentlemen, The First Noël, The Holly and the Ivy* cycle out at the same manic pace as the organ-grinder turns his handle and holds out his black velvet bag.

"Merry Christmas! Merry Christmas!" His hat is covered in melting snow but his arm moves the crank with the same disciplined regularity it's turned for forty years or more. *Away in a Manger. Good King Wenceslas. O, Tannenbaum. O, Tannenbaum. Silent Night. Rudolf the Red-Nosed Reindeer.* Cathy puts a half-penny in his hat for luck, but Jerry's never known his luck to change one way or another from giving anything to the barrel organ man. He pulls Cathy's hand for fear her generosity will beggar them. "Come on. We'll do that butcher right at the top. Then we'll work our way down." There's no such thing as a frozen turkey here. Not in any Portobello butcher's worth the name, and all the veg is fresh from Covent Garden. All the fruit is there for the handling, though the stall-holders affect shocked disgust when the middle-class women, copying French models, reach to feel. "No need for that, love. It's all fresh. Don't worry, darling, it won't get any harder if you squeeze it." Dirty laughter does the trick. "Ha, ha, ha!" Gin and best bitter add nuance to the innuendo. Panatella smoke drifts from the warm pubs. Chestnuts roast and pop on red-hot oil-drum braziers.

And Jerry looks behind him. "It was all true," he says. "It really was. Every Christmas after the Blitz."

"Well, possibly." Miss Brunner's attention was on the present. The box was big enough at any rate, in red, gold, and green shining paper and a spotted black and white bow. "Nothing beats Christmas for horrible colour combinations."

"Of course, it couldn't last." Jerry contemplated the best way of opening the present without messing up the wrapping. "The snow, I mean. Turned to sleet almost immediately. By the time we got to our place at eighty-seven Ladbroke Grove, with the turkey, it was pelting down rain. I had to go back for the tree. At least I could hold it over my head on the way home." He'd opened it. The brown cardboard box was revealed, covered in black and blue printed legends and specifications. Automatically, neatly, he folded the wrapping. He beamed his appreciation, his fingers caressing the familiar sans-serif brand name in bars of red, white, and blue. "Oh, *blimey!* A new Banning."

Shakey Mo Collier grinned through his scrubby beard. "I got another for myself at the same time. Joe's Guns had a two-for-one."

Using a Mackintosh chair she'd found, Miss Brunner had built a blaze in the ornamental grate. Smoke and cinders were blowing everywhere. "There's nothing like a fire on Christmas morning." She drew back the heavy Morris curtains. There was a touch of grey in the black sky. Somewhere a motor grunted and shuffled. "Don't worry," she said. "I think it's dead."

Carefully, Jerry peeled the scotch tape from the box. The number in big letters was beside a picture of the gun itself: BM-152A. He reached in and drew out a ziplock full of heavy clips. "Oh, God! Ammo included." His eyes were touched with silver. "I don't deserve friends like you."

"Shall we get started?" Miss Brunner smoothed the skirt of her tweed two-piece, indicating the three identical Gent's Royal

Albert bicycles she'd brought up from the basement. "We're running out of time."

"Back to good old sixty-two." Mo smacked his lips. "Even earlier, if we pedal fast enough. OK, me old mucker. Strap that thing on and let's go go go!"

They wheeled their bikes out through the side door of the V&A into Exhibition Road. White flakes settled on the shoulders of Jerry's black car coat. He knew yet another thrill of delight. "Snow!"

"Don't be silly," she said. "Ash."

With a certain sadness Jerry swung the Banning on his back then threw his leg over the saddle. He was happy to be leaving the future.

2. WHEN DID SUNNIS START FIGHTING SHIITES?

> Scanning your brain while you watch horror movies might hold the key to making them even more frightening. The findings could reshape the way scary movies—perhaps all movies—are filmed.
>
> —*Popular Science*, June 2010

THE HOLIDAYS OVER, Jerry Cornelius stepped off the Darfur jet and set his watch for 1962. Time to go home. At least this wouldn't be as hairy as last time. He'd had a close shave on the plane. His head was altogether smoother now.

Shakey Mo and Major Nye met him at the checkout. Shakey rattled his new keys. "Where to, chief?" He was already getting into character.

Major Nye wasn't comfortable with the Hummer. It was ostentatious and far too strange for the times. He might as well be driving a Model T, he got so much attention.

"I hate it," said Jerry. "And not in a good way."

Resignedly, Major Nye let Mo take the Westway exit. "A military vehicle should be just that. A civilian vehicle should be suitable for civilian roads. This is a kind of jeep, what?" He had never liked jeeps for some reason. Even Land Rovers weren't his cup of tea. He had enjoyed the old Duesenberg or the green Lagonda. To disguise his disapproval he sang fragments of his favourite music hall songs. "*A little of what you fancy does you good . . . My old man said follow the van . . . Don't you think my dress is a little bit, just a little bit, not too much of it . . . With a pair of opera glasses, you could see to Hackney Marshes, if it wasn't for the houses in between . . .*"

"So how was the genocide, boss?" Mo was well pleased, as if the years of isolation had never been. He patted his big Mark 8 on the seat beside him and rearranged the ammo pods. "Going well?"

"A bit disappointing." Jerry looked out at grey London roofs. He smiled, remembering his mum. All he needed was a touch of drizzle.

"*Heaven, I'm in heaven . . .*" began Major Nye, shifting into Fred Astaire. "Oh Bugger!" Mo started inching into the new Shepherds Bush turn-off. The major would be glad to see this American heap returned to the garage so he could start dusting off the yellow Commer as soon as Mr. Trux came back from his holidays. Thank god it was only rented. Mo, of course, had wanted to buy one. Over in the next century Karl Lagerfeld was selling his. A sure sign the vehicles were out of fashion. They drove between the dull brick piles of the Notting Dale housing estates whose architecture was designed to soak up all the city's misery and reflect it. Major Nye glanced at Jerry. With his '60s car coat and knitted white scarf, his shaven head, Jerry resembled a released French convict, some Vautrin back from the past to claim his revenge. Actually, of course, he was returning to the past to pay what remained of his dues. He'd had enough of revenge. He had appeared, it was said, in West London in 1960, the offspring of a Notting Hill Gate greengrocer and a South London music hall performer. But who really knew? He had spent almost his whole existence as a self-invented myth.

Major Nye knew for certain that Mrs. Cornelius had died at a ripe age in a Blenheim Crescent basement in 1976. At least, it might have been 1976. Possibly '77. Her "boyfriend," as she called him, Pyat, the old Polish second-hand clothes dealer, had died in the same year. A heart attack. It had been a bit of a tragic time, all in all. Four years later, Jerry had left, been killed and resurrected countless times, went missing. After that, Nye had stopped visiting London. He was glad he had spent most of his life in the country. The climate was much healthier.

As Mo steered into the mews the major approvingly noted that the cobbles were back. Half the little cul-de-sac was still stables with Dutch doors. Mo got out to undo the lockup where they had arranged to leave the car. Nye could tell from the general condition of the place, with its flaking nondescript paint and stink of mould and manure, that they were already as good as home. From somewhere in the back of the totters yard came the rasp of old cockney, the stink of drunkard's sweat. It had to be Jerry's Uncle Edmund. That cawing might be the distant *kar-har-kaa* of crows or an old man's familiar cough.

Major Nye could not be sure he was actually home but it was clear that the others were certain. This was their natural environment. From somewhere came the aroma of vinegar-soaked newspaper, limp chips.

3. CAPTAIN MARVEL BATTLES HIS OWN CONSCIENCE!!!!!

> Knowing that we are slaves of our virtual histories, the soldiers play dice beneath the cross. A bloody spear leans against the base. A goblet and a piece of good cloth are to be won. "What's that?" says a soldier, hearing a groan overhead. "Nothing." His companion rattles the dice in his cupped hands. "Something about his father."
>
> —Michel LeBriard, *Les Nihilists*

"UP TO YOUR old tricks, eh, Mr. Cornelius?" Miss Brunner adjusted her costume. "Well, they won't work here."

"They never did work. You just had the illusion of effect. But you said it yourself, Miss B—*follow the money*. You can't change the economics. You can just arrange the window dressing a bit."

"Sez you!" Shakey Mo fingered his gun's elaborate instrumentation. "There's a bullet in here with your address on it."

Birmingham had started to burn. The reflected flames gave a certain liveliness to Miss Brunner's features. "Now look what you've done!"

"It doesn't matter." Jerry rubbed at his itching skull. "They'll never make anything out of it. I must be off."

She sniffed. "Yes. That explains everything."

She wobbled a little on her ultra-high heels as she reboarded the chopper. "Where to next?"

4. ECCE RUMPO

All Nazis fear The Yellow Star,
Who leaves his card upon the bar.
And 'scaping from their railroad car
He's gone again, the Yellow Star!

—Lafarge and Taylor, *The Adventures of the Yellow Star,* 1941

JERRY WAS SURPRISED to see his dad's faux Le Corbusier chateau in such good shape, considering the beating it had taken over the years. Obviously someone had kept it up. In spite of the driving rain and the mud, the place looked almost welcoming.

Mo took a proprietal pleasure in watching Jerry's face. "Maintenance is what I've always been into. Everything that isn't original is a perfect repro. Even those psychedelic towers your dad was so keen on. He was ahead of his time, your dad. He practically invented acid. Not to mention acid rain. And we all know how far ahead of his time he was with computers." Mo sighed. "He was a baby badly waiting for the microchip. If he'd lived." He blinked reflectively and studied the curved metal casings of his Banning, fingering the ammo clips and running the flat of his hand over the long, tapering barrel. "He understood machinery, your dad. He lived for it. The Leo IV was his love. He built that house for machinery."

"And these days all he'd need for the same thing would be a speck or two of dandruff." Miss Brunner passed her hand through her tight perm and then looked suspiciously at her nails. "Can we go in?" She sat down on the chopper's platform and started pulling her thick wellies up her leg.

High above them, against the dark beauty of the night, a rocket streaked, its intense red tail burning like a ruby.

Jerry laughed. "I thought all that was over."

"Nothing's over." She sighed. "Nothing's ever bloody over."

Mo remembered why he disliked her.

They began to trudge through the clutching mud which oozed around them. Melting chocolate.

"Bloody global warming," said Jerry.

"You should have concentrated harder, Mr. C."

He didn't hear her. In his mind he was eyeless in Gaza at the doors of perception.

5. THE WANTON OF ARGOS

> People claim that Portugal is an island. They say that you can't get there without wetting your feet. They say all those tales concerning dusty border roads into Spain are mere fables.
>
> —Geert Mak, *In Europe*, 2004

UP AT THE far end of the hall Miss Brunner was enjoying an Abu Ghraib moment. The screams were getting on all their nerves. Jerry turned up *Pidgin English* by Elvis Costello but nothing worked the way it should any more. He had systematically searched his father's house while Miss Brunner applied electrodes to his brother Frank's tackle. "Was this really what the '60s were all about?" he mused.

"Oh, God," said Frank. "Oh, bloody hell." He'd never looked very good naked. Too pale. Too skinny. But ready to talk:

"You think you're going to find the secret of the '60s in a fake French modernist villa built by a barmy lapsed papist romantic Jew who went through World War II in a trench coat and wincyette pajamas fucking every sixty-a-day bereaved or would-be bereaved middle-class Englishwoman who ever got a first at Cambridge, who was fucked by a communist and who claimed that deddy had never wanted her to be heppy? Not exactly rock and roll, is it, Jerry. You'd be better off questioning your old mum. The Spirit of the bloody Blitz." He sniffed. "Is that Bar-B-Q?"

"They all had the jazz habit." Jerry was defensive. "They all knew the blues."

"Oh, quite." Miss Brunner was disgusted. "Jack Parnell and his Gentleman Jazzers at the Café de Paris. Or was it Chris Barber and his Skiffling Sidemen?"

"Skiffle," said Jerry, casting around for his washboard. "The Blue Men. The Square Men. The Quarry Men. The Green Horns. The Black Labels. The Red Barrels."

"You ought to be ashamed of yourself," said Mo. He was rifling through the debris, looking for some antique ammo clips. "Someone went to a lot of trouble to bring this place over, stone by stone, to Ladbroke Grove. Though, I agree, it's a shame about the Hearst Castle."

"It was always more suitable for Hastings." Miss Brunner stared furiously at Jerry's elastic-sided Cubans. "You're going to ruin those shoes, if you're not careful."

"It's not cool to be careful," he said. "Remember, this is the '60s. You haven't won yet. Careful is the '80s. Entirely different."

"Is this the Gibson?" Mo had found the guitar behind a mould-grown library desk.

Miss Brunner went back to working on Frank.

"The Gibson?" Jerry spoke hopefully. But when he checked, it was the wrong number.

"Can I have it, then?" asked Mo.
Jerry shrugged.

6. WILLIAM'S CROWDED HOUR

> . . . and does anyone know what "the flip side" was? It was from the days when gramophone records were double-sided. You played your 78 rpm or your 33 1/3 or your 45 and then you turned it over and played the other side. Only nostalgia dealers and vinyl freaks remember that stuff now.
>
> —Maurice Little, *Down the Portobello*, 2007

CHRISTMAS 1962, SNOW still falling. Reports said there was no end in sight. Someone on the Third Program even suggested a new Ice Age had started. At dawn, Jerry left his flat in Lancaster Gate, awakened by the tolling of bells from the church tower almost directly in line with his window, and went out into Hyde Park. His were the first footprints in the snow. It felt like sacrilege. Above him, crows circled. He told himself they were calling to him. He knew them all by name. They were reluctant to land, but then he saw their black clawprints as he got closer to the Serpentine. The prints were beginning to fill up. He wondered if the birds would follow him again. He planned to go over to Ladbroke Grove and take the presents to his mum and the others. But first he had to visit Mrs. Pash and listen to the player piano for old time's sake. They always got their Schoenberg rolls out for Christmas Day.

A crone appeared from behind a large chestnut. She wore a big red coat with a hood, trimmed in white, and she carried a basket. Jerry recognized her; but, to humour her, he pretended to be surprised as she approached.

"Good luck, dear," she said. "You've got almost seven years left. And seven's a lucky number, isn't it?" She wrapped her lilac chiffon round her scrawny throat. Ersatz syrup. Somewhere drums and motorcycle engines began to beat. "Seven years!"

Jerry knew better. "Twenty-two years and some months according to the SS. Owning your misery is the quickest way of getting out from under. What will happen to individualism under the law?"

"Obama will change all that, darling. Great lawyers are coming. They will change corporations into individuals. Cross my palm with silver and I'll tell you the future. Cross it with gold and I'll explain the present."

Checking his watches, Jerry smiled and turned up the collar of his black car coat. He put one gloved hand on the Roller's gear stick, another on the wheel. He was still searching for his Dornier DoX seaplanes. Last he'd looked Catherine had been aboard.

"What's the time? My watches stopped."

7. HOW TO GET YOUR FREE STATE $2 BILLS

> When asked to imagine the Earth in 2040, many scientists describe a grim scenario, a landscape so bare and dry it's almost uninhabitable. But that's not what Willem van Cottem sees. "It will be a green world," says van Cottem, a Belgian scientist turned social entrepreneur. "Tropical fruit can grow wherever it's warm. You still need water, but not much. A brief splash of rain every once in a while is enough. And voila—from sandy soil, lush gardens grow. The secret is hydrogels, powerfully absorbent polymers that can suck up hundreds of times their weight in water. Hydrogels have many applications today, from food processing to mopping up oil spills, but they are most familiar as the magic ingredient in disposable diapers.
>
> —*Popular Science*, July 2010

"BELONGING, JERRY, IS very important to me." Colonel Pyat glanced up and down the deserted Portobello. Crows were hopping about in the gutters. Old newspapers, scraps of lettuce, squashed tomatoes, ruined apples. Even the scavengers, their ragged forms moving methodically up and down the street, rejected them.

Jerry looked over at the cinema. The Essoldo was showing three pictures for 1/6d. *Mrs. Miniver*, *The Winslow Boy*, and *Brief Encounter*.

"Heppy deddy?" he asked no-one in particular.

"There you are!" The colonel was triumphant. "You can speak perfectly properly if you want to!"

Jerry was disappointed. He had expected a different triple feature. He had been told it would be *Epic Hero and the Beast*, *First Spaceship on Venus*, and *Forbidden Planet*.

"Rets!" he said.

8. A GAME OF PATIENCE

> Art, which should be the unique preoccupation of the privileged few, has become a general rule . . . A fashion . . . A furor . . . artism!
>
> —Felix Pyat

"THERE'S ALWAYS A bridge somewhere." Mo paced up and down the levee like a neurotic dog. Every few minutes he licked his lips with his long red tongue. At other times he stood stock-still staring inland, upriver. From the gloom came the sound of a riverboat's groaning wail, and an exchange of shouts between pilots over their bullhorns. Heavy waves of black liquid crashed against hulls. The words were impossible to make out, like cops ordering traffic, but nobody cared what they were saying. Further downriver, from what remained of the city, came the mock-carousel music inviting visitors to a showboat whose paddles, splashing like the vanes of a ruined windmill, stuck high out of filthy brown water full of empty Evian and Ozarka bottles.

Further upstream, scavengers with empty cans were trying to skim thick oil off the surface.

Jerry called up from the water. He had found a raft and was poling it slowly to the gently curving concrete level. "Mo. Throw down a rope!"

"The Pope? We haven't got a pope." Mo was confused.

"A rope!"

"We going to hang him?"

Jerry gave up and let the raft drift back into midstream. He sat down in the centre, his gun stuck up between his spread legs.

"You going to town?" Mo wanted to know.

When Jerry didn't answer, he began to pad slowly along the levee, following the creak of the raft in the water, the shadow that he guessed to be his friend's. From somewhere in the region of Jackson Square vivid red, white, and blue neon flickered on and off before it was again extinguished. Then the sun set, turning the water a beautiful, bloody crimson. The broken towers along St. Charles Street appeared in deep silhouette for a few moments and disappeared in the general darkness. The voices of the pilots stopped suddenly and all Mo could hear was the sullen lapping of the river.

"Jerry?"

Later, Mo was relieved at the familiar razz—a kazoo playing a version of "Alexander's Ragtime Band." He looked up and down. "Is that you?"

Jerry had always been fond of Berlin.

9. PAKISTAN – THE TALIBAN TAKEOVER

> A mysterious young man met at luncheon
> Said "My jaws are so big I can munch on
> A horse and a pig and a ship in full rig
> And my member's the size of a truncheon."
> —Maurice LeB, 1907

MONSTROUS HOVERING BATTLE CRUISERS cast black shadows over half a mile in all directions when Jerry finally reached the field, his armoured Lotus HMV VII's batteries all but exhausted. He would have to abandon the vehicle and hope to get back to Exeter with the cavalry, assuming there was still a chance to make peace and assuming there still was an Exeter. He leapt from the vehicle and ran towards the tent where the Cornish commander had set up his headquarters.

The cool air moaned with the soft noise of idling motors. Cornish forces, including Breton and Basque allies, covered the moors on four sides of the Doone valley, the sound of their vast camp all but silenced by its understanding of the force brought against it. Imperial Germany, Burgundy, and Catalonia had joined Hannover to crush this final attempt to restore Tudor power and return the British capital to Cardiff.

Even as Jerry reached the royal tent, Queen Jennifer stepped out, a vision in mirrored steel, acknowledging his deep bow. Her captains crowded behind her, anxious for information.

"Do you, my lord, bring news from Poole?" She was pale, straight-backed, ever beautiful. He cared as much for her extraordinary posture as any of her other qualities. Were they still lovers?

"Poole has fallen, your majesty, while the Isle of Wight lies smouldering and extinguished. Even Barnstaple's great shipyards are destroyed. We reckoned, my lady, without the unsentimental severity of Hannover's fleet. We have only cavalry and infantry remaining."

"Your own family?"

"Your majesty, I sent them to sanctuary in the Scillies."

She turned away, hiding her expression from him.

Her voice was steady when it addressed her commanders. "Gentlemen, you may return to your homes. The day is already lost and I would not see you die in vain." She turned to Jerry, murmuring: "And what of Gloucester?"

"The same, my lady."

A tear showed now in her calm, beautiful eyes. Yet her voice remained steady. "Then we are all defeated. I'll spill no more senseless blood. Tell Hannover I will come to London by July's end. Take this to him." Slowly, with firm hands, she unbuckled her sword.

10. THE EPIC SEARCH FOR A TECH HERO

> The penalties in France will be much higher than in Belgium. The fine for a first offence will be €150. And a man who is found to have forced a woman to wear a full-length veil will be punished with a fine of €15,000 and face imprisonment. The crackdown on the veil has come from the very top of the political establishment, with President Sarkozy declaring that the burqa is "not welcome" in France and denouncing it as a symbol of female "subservience and debasement."
>
> —*New Statesman*, May 31, 2010

MARIA AMIS, JULIA Barnes, and Iona MacEwan, the greatest lady novelists of their day, were taking tea at Liberty one afternoon in the summer of 2011. They had all been close friends at Girton in the same class and had shared many adventures. As time passed their fortunes prospered and their interests changed, to such a degree, in fact, that on occasion they had "had words" and spent almost a decade out of direct communication; but now, in middle years, they were reconciled. *Love's Arrow* had won the Netta Musket Award; *The Lime Sofa*, the Ouida Prize; and *Under Alum Chine*, the Barbara Cartland Memorial Prize. All regularly topped the bestseller lists.

In their expensive but unshowy summer frocks and hats, they were a vision of civilized femininity.

The tea rooms had recently been redecorated in William Morris 'Willow Pattern,' and brought a refreshing lightness to their surroundings. The lady novelists enjoyed a sense of secure content which they had not known since their Cambridge days.

The satisfaction of this cosy moment was only a little spoiled by the presence of a young man with bright shoulder-length black hair, dark blue eyes, long, regular features, and a rather athletic physique, wearing a white shirt, black car coat, and narrow, dark grey trousers, with pointed "Cuban" elastic-sided boots, who sat in the corner nearest to the door. Occasionally, he would look up from his teacakes and darjeeling and offer them a friendly, knowing wink.

"And should we feel concern for the Irish?" Iona determinedly asked the table. She had always nursed an interest in politics.

"*Cherchez l'argent*," reflected Maria.

Thinking this vulgar, Julia looked for the waitress.

11. LES FAUX MONNAYEURS

> Things were happening as we motored into Ypres. When were they not? A cannonade of sorts behind the roofless ruins, perhaps outside of town; nobody seems to know or care; only an air-fight for our benefit. We crane our necks and train our glasses. Nothing whatever to be seen.
>
> —E. W. Hornung, *New Statesman*, June 30, 1917

> The buying power of the proletariat's gone down
> Our money's getting shallow and weak.
>
> —Bob Dylan, *Modern Times*, 2006

JERRY'S HEAD TURNED on the massive white pillow and he saw something new in his sister's trust even as she slipped into his arms, her soft comfort warming him. "You'll be leaving, then?" she asked.

"I catch the evening packet from Canterbury. By tonight I'll be in Paris. There's still time to think again."

"I must stay here." Her breathing became more rapid. "But I promise I'll join you if the cryogenics . . ." Her voice broke. "By Christmas. Oh, Jesus, Jerry. It's tragic. I love you."

His expression puzzled her, he knew. He had dreamed of her lying in her coffin while an elaborate funeral went on around her. He remembered her in both centuries. Image after image came back to him, confusing in their intensity and clarity. It was almost unbearable. Why had he always loved her with such passion? Such complete commitment? That old feeling. Of course, she had not been the only woman he had loved so unselfconsciously, so deeply, but she was the only one to reciprocate with the same depth and commitment. The only one to last his lifetime. The texture of her short, brown hair reminded him of Jenny. Of Jenny's friend, Eve. Of the pleasures the three of them had shared through much of the '70s when Catherine was away with Una Persson . . .

Looking over Eve's head through copper hot eyes as her friend moved her beautiful full lips over his penis, Jenny's face bore that expression of strong affection which was the nearest she came to love. His fingers clung deep in Eve's long dark hair, his mouth on Jenny's as she frigged herself. The subtle differences of skin shades; their eye colours. The graceful movements. That extraordinary passion. Jenny's lips parted and small delicious grunts came from her mouth. This was almost the last of what the '60s had brought them and which most other generations could never enjoy: pleasure without conflict or fear of serious consequences; the most exquisite form of lust. Meanwhile, taking such deep humane pleasure in the love of the moment, Jerry could not know (though he had begun to guess) what the future would bring. And were his actions, which felt so innocent, the cause of the horror, which would within two decades begin to fill the whole world?

"Was it my fault?" he asked her.

She sat up, smiling. "Look at the time!"

12. HOME ALONE FIVE

> I learned from Taguba that the first wave of materials included descriptions of the sexual humiliation of a father with his son, who were both detainees. Several of these images, including one of an Iraqi woman detainee baring her breasts, have since surfaced; others have not. (Taguba's report noted that photographs and videos were being held by the C.I.D. because of ongoing criminal investigations and their "extremely sensitive nature.") Taguba said that he saw "a video

of a male American soldier in uniform sodomizing a female detainee." The video was not made public in any of the subsequent court proceedings, nor has there been any public government mention of it. Such images would have added an even more inflammatory element to the outcry over Abu Ghraib. "It's bad enough that there were photographs of Arab men wearing women's panties," Taguba said.

—Seymour M. Hersh, "The General's Report," *New Yorker*, June 25, 2007.

PORTOBELLO ROAD, DESERTED except for a few stallholders setting up before dawn, had kept its familiar Friday morning atmosphere. As Jerry approached the Westway, one hand deep in the pocket of his black car coat, the other still in its black glove resting on the handlebars of his Gent's Royal Albert bicycle, he glanced at the big neon NEW WORLDS Millennium clock, in vivid red and blue, erected to celebrate the magazine's fifty-fifth birthday. Two doors closer to the bridge, and not yet open, were the *FRENDZ* offices, and nearby were *Time Out*, Rough Trade, Stiff Records International, Riviera Management, Mac's Music, Trux Transportation, Stone's Antiquarian Books, Pash's Instruments, The Mountain Grill, Brock and Turner, The Mandrake, Smilin' Mike's Club; all the great names which had made the Grove famous and given the area its enduring character.

"I remember when I used to be a denizen round here. Glad to see the old neighbourhood has kept going." Jerry spoke to his friend, Professor Hira, who had remained behind when the others had gone away.

"Only by a whisker," said the plump Brahmin, shaking his head. "By a lot of hard work and visionary thinking on the part of those of us who didn't leave."

Jerry began to smile; clearly Hira was overpraising himself and being slightly judgmental at the same time. But Hira was serious: "Believe me, old boy, I'm not blaming you for going. You had a different destiny. But you don't know what it's like out there any more. North Kensington is all that remains of the free world. Roughly east of Queensway, north of Harrow Road, south of Holland Park Avenue, west of Wood Lane, a new kind of tyranny triumphs."

"It can't be much worse than it was!"

"Oh, that's what we all thought in 1975 or so. We hadn't, even then, begun to realize what Fate—or anyway The City—had in store for us. Ladbroke Grove is the only part of Britain which managed to resist the march of the Whiteshirts from out of the suburbs. We keep the night alive with our signs. That's a battle we're constantly fighting. Thank god we still have a few people with money *and* conscience. All the work we did in the '60s and '70s, to maintain the freeholds and rents successfully kept the Grove in the hands of the original inhabitants, so that, at worst, we are a living museum of the Golden Age. At our best, we have slowed time long enough for people to take stock, not to be panicked or threatened by the Whiteshirts. Here, the wealth is still evenly distributed, continuing the progress made between 1920 and 1970. And through the insistence of our ancient charters, the Grove, along with Brookgate in the east, like London's ancient Alsacia, has managed to keep her status as an independent state, a sanctuary."

"Ruritania, eh? I thought the air smelled a bit stale."

"Well, we've developed recycling to a bit of a fine art. Out there in the rest of the country, as in the USA, where the majority of the wealth was encouraged by Thatcher and her colleagues to flow back to Capital, things of course are considerably worse for the greater middle class. Thatcher and her kind used all the power put into their hands by short-sighted unions and their far-sighted opponents. Every threat. Every technique. Those who resisted made themselves helpless by refusing to change their rhetoric and so were also unable to change their strategies. It's true, old boy. For thirty years the outside world has collapsed into cynicism as the international conglomerates became big enough to challenge, then control and finally replace elected governments. You're lucky you were brought back here, Mr. C. Outside, it's pretty unpleasant, I can tell you. Most

Londoners can't afford to live where they were born. *Colons* from the suburbs or worse, the country, have flooded in, taking over our houses, our businesses, our restaurants and shops. Of course, it was starting in your time: George Melly and stripped pine shops. But now the working class is strictly confined to its ghettoes, distracted by drugs, lifestyle magazines and reality TV. The middle class has been trained to compete tooth and nail for the advantages they once took for granted, and the rich do whatever they like, including murder, thanks to their obscene amounts of moolah." Even Hira's language appeared to have been frozen in the period of his dog years. "At least the middle class learned to value what they had taken for granted, even if it's too late to do anything about it now!"

"Bloody hell," said Jerry. "It looks like I was better off in that other future, after all. And now I've burned my bridges. Who's Thatcher?"

"We call her The Goddess Miggea. Most of them worship her today, though she was the one who formulated the language used to place the middle class in its present unhappy position. She was a sort of quisling for the Whiteshirts. She's the main symbol of middle class downfall, yet they still think she saved them, the way the Yanks think Reagan got them out of trouble. Amazing, isn't it. You said yourself that the secret of successful feudalism is to make the peasants believe it's the best of all possible worlds. Blair and Bush thought they could reproduce those successes with a brief war against a weak nation, but they miscalculated rather badly. Too late now. The personalities have changed. Remember the old scenario for nuclear war which put Pakistan at the centre of the picture? Well, it's not far off. Religion's back with a vengeance. I'd return to India, only things aren't much better there. You probably haven't heard of Hindu Nationalism, either. Or the Mombai Tiger. The rich are so much richer and the poor are so much poorer. The rich have no sense of charity or gravitas. They enjoy the power and the extravagance of 18th century French aristocrats. They distract themselves with all kinds of speculative adventures, including wars, which make

Vietnam seem idealistic. How the people of Eastern Europe mourn the fall of the old Soviet empire, nostalgic for the return of the certainties of tyranny! Am I boring you, Mr. Cornelius?"

"Sorry." Jerry was admiring a massive plasma TV in an electrical shop's display window. "Wow! The future's got everything we hoped it would have! The Soviet Union's fallen?"

"I forget. I suppose that in your day so much of this seemed impossible, or at least unlikely. Thirty-five years ago you were talking about zero population growth and the problem of leisure. Here we are at the new Smaller Business Bureau. Lovely, isn't it? Yes, I know, it smells like Amsterdam. I work here now." Carefully, he opened the doors of Reception.

13. OFFSHORE OPERATIONS

> "Carbon neutral" sounds pretty straightforward—simply remove as much carbon from the atmosphere as you put in. The trouble is civilization began emitting CO_2 when humans burned the first lump of coal about 4,000 years ago.
>
> —*Popular Science*, July 2010

"I THOUGHT YOU were an ally." Jerry tucked his shirt into his chinos and swung down from the examination couch. No?"

Dr. Didi Dee looked up from beneath furious brows. "Why should I be now?" She assumed a frozen defence. "Now I'm a missionary? A Christian?"

Jerry's mum heard this. She had forced him to keep this appointment and almost forced him to come. She was looking tired, even for her age. "But you were a Christian before, weren't you, dear? Before poor old Obarmy, I mean."

"Don't refer to our President like that."

"Sorry, love. I forgot what gods yer always puttin' up, you Yanks. No offence. Personally I don't know wot yer see in 'im, long streak a piss."

"It's all right, mum." Jerry didn't like her timing. "It's just authority. They love it. They're even pre-Biblical sometimes. Poor old Moses. Talk about idolatory."

"Now you're being spiteful." Dr. Didi Dee was grim again. "I'm the one with the prescription pad. Are you going to do as I tell you or not?"

"It's the German influence, I think." Mrs. Cornelius was trying out the umbrella she had brought with her from Sri Lanka. "It's not because you're black, dearie, is it? I had a friend like you. Well, not as pretty, admittedly. But not in this day and age, surely?"

"Get her out of here." Didi Dee folded her arms under her breasts. "And I'd get out of town, if I were you."

"Oh, bugger." Jerry rubbed at a small scab on his wrist. "I thought this was too good to be true. So what's it about?"

"It's about Obarmy, dear, isn't it? We're all disappointed. It's not just you."

Mrs. Cornelius had become a little spiteful since her recent resurrection, thought Jerry. There were subtleties to American society mysterious to most Europeans. They thought they knew what was going on, but really they had absolutely no idea. They mocked Americans for not knowing where Prague was and didn't know how to pronounce Houston. Jerry wondered if the country would be any better if the French had beaten the British. Or if Tom Paine's Parliament had been permitted. Well, there was no point in going to Mississippi now: now that he knew Cathy/Colinda wasn't there. Maybe Louisiana? And then Texas? He'd like to see the Gulf again, if only to take a gamble on the boats, risk his all at The Terminal Café. *La mer d'huile Mes jolies, mes corazoa, deux pieds assayez langue du gringo, meyenherren.* How can we stop all this?

He began to laugh at last.

14. CHASING A CURE

> When it comes to internal rules for the U.S. military, the Obama administration is not going to be wishy-washy. The armed forces will be given, well, marching orders.
>
> —*Northeast Mississippi Daily Journal: A Locally Owned Newspaper Dedicated to the Service of God and Mankind*, June 15, 2010

IT WON'T BE LONG, Major Nye thought of telling his captors, before the public become confused and bewildered and that's when they got to be radical activists. So which came first, the golden egg or Mother Goose? But he saw no point in voicing this question. The kidnappers had been courteous to a fault and he had no wish to trouble them with his own problems. Nonetheless, he was beginning to wonder if he shouldn't have taken them to a French farce first.

The orchestra grew louder, anticipating the coming scenes. Clown crept comically across the stage, a long string of sausages trailing from his pocket, the huge golden egg clutched to his splendid chest. Alerted by the music, he stared nervously around him, trying to stuff the egg into his pocket, to hide the sausages.

Where was Columbine? Could she save him again?

The limelight found Harlequin, following him as he danced across the stage, admired himself in the mirror, then dived through it, discovering with amazement the fantastic world of the future where mounted highwaymen held up trams on Hampstead Heath and were pursued by Bow Street Runners.

15. A NIGHT TO REMEMBER

> Artificial clouds, flocks of jet packs, carbon emissions turned back into gasoline—it all sounds a little crazy, but the people behind these ideas are the bold thinkers who could save the planet. Plus: not everyone can be a visionary.
>
> —*Popular Science*, July 2010

HOW SAD TO be back in Simla as the rainy season ended, and an ice age was yet to begin. Jerry looked for his old nanny, his governess, his uncle in his gorgeous uniform, but they appeared to have gone ahead. He watched a lazy flotilla of civil airships bringing holiday-makers back from Nepal and Ever Rest.

"Goodbye." He straightened his Panama on his raven waves. It would be strange to see the old place taken over by developers. Major Nye had been close to tears, but Jerry had nothing to feel nostalgia for, not really. Just race memory he supposed of Victorian novels, Sexton Blake stories, John Ford movies, and all that Jewel in the Skull romancery. He had never wanted it back but he had wanted to retain the fiction, the escape. Major Nye had been its finest creation. The visionary patriarch who saw Modern India rising from the ruins of religion and barbaric tradition. Thank god the major wasn't in the position of the many poor devils stranded between India A&M missing the power and the swagger of it all.

Didi looked glamorous in her scarlet and yellow sari, and she had mellowed a bit, gliding her long fingers between his arm and his torso, coupling. Jerry wasn't too easy with this. He let her fingers curl onto his arm but his body withdrew somehow. "You must miss it," she whispered.

"Not this time," he promised. "This time I'll hit it."

A black oriental cat, tail erect, rubbed itself against his leg. He bent to pick it up.

She was weeping. She felt around in her purse and found a handkerchief, a bottle of smelling salts, some Kleenex.

"Bloody allergies." It was a request. "I'd forgotten all about that."

He raised the cat in his arms, stroking it. "What?"

She shuddered at his cruelty. "Obedient girls."

He winked.

"You're addicted to the dosh, aren't you? Is that why you joined the Baptists?"

16. BIGGLES: THE LIMITED EDITIONS

> Sixty years after the famous outdoor writer Nash Buckingham lost his beloved shotgun after a duck hunt in Arkansas, a highly-anticipated auction delivers the beautiful Fox 12-gauge to its final resting place.
>
> —*Garden and Gun* magazine, June/July 2010

JERRY WAS BACK in Panto playing Clown to his brother Frank's Harlequin. As usual, Cathy was Columbine. Jerry had Grimaldi's vegetable monster routine pretty much perfected. The orchestra struck up, all drums, cymbals, and brass, as Harlequin drew his slapstick and chopped the monster to bits before Clown's widening eyes.

But Sadlers Wells wasn't the place it had been, thought Major Nye, who hoped he was offering moral support by coming to this dress rehearsal. He had persuaded his captors to make the exchange here. He hated breaking promises and, as old school mobsmen, they respected that.

The scenery was perhaps too familiar. The big trick numbers, the magic and transformation business, all had a bit of a tawdry look. Major Nye had an idea that the public recognized what that revealed but kept coming anyway, missing the richness of shades and forms still unrecognized by an academia preferring a macrocosm and simplicity rather than complexity. It won't be long, he had told his captors, before the public became confused and bewildered and that's when they produced radical activists. Of course, even the Cornelius family, as old as the Grimaldis, the Lupinos, and the Lanes, were hardly aware of the deep tradition they reflected.

"We're running late." The big, old wrestler, a Greek, put gentle fingers on Major Nye's arm. He had the ransom money in a brown paper carrier bag. "We'll be on our way, major. You won't mind us not standing on ceremony, will you? We were expected back in Bayswater half an hour ago."

"Not a bit, old boy. Mind how you drive." The major tried to stand but he was numb all over.

The Greek shook his head, gesturing for him to remain seated.

For the first time Major Nye noticed that the two heavy, somewhat overdressed men, were sweating.

He felt grateful to them and a little proud that at his age he could still fetch a good price.

The limelight fell on Jerry stepping to the front of the stage to reprise his tribute to Joey Grimaldi:

"Lastly, be jolly, be alive, be light,
Twitch, flirt and caper, tumble, fall and throw,
Grow up right ugly in thy father's sight,
And be an 'absolute Joseph,' like old Joe."

KATRINA, KATRINA!

> It fell to Neville Chamberlain in one of the supreme crises of the world to be contradicted by events, to be disappointed in his hopes, and to be deceived and cheated by a wicked man. But what were these hopes in which he was disappointed? What were these wishes in which he was frustrated? What was the faith that was abused? They were among the most noble instincts of the human heart—the love of peace, the strife for peace, the pursuit of peace, even at great peril and certainly to the utter disdain of popularity or clamor.
>
> —Winston Churchill to Parliament, November 12, 1940

1. WHY YOU SHOULD FEAR PRESIDENT GIULIANI

> Parts of rural China are seeing a burgeoning market for female corpses, the result of the reappearance of a strange custom called "ghost marriages." Chinese tradition demands that husbands and wives always share a grave. Sometimes when a man died unmarried, his parents would procure the body of a woman, hold a "wedding" and bury the couple together.
>
> —*The Economist*, July 28, 2007

"THERE ARE NO more sanctuaries, m'sieur. You are probably too young even to dream of such things. But I grew up with the idea that, I don't know, you could retire to a little cottage in the country or find a deserted beach somewhere or a cabin in the mountains. Now we're lucky if we can get an apartment in Nice, enough equity in it to pay for the extra healthcare we'll need." Monsieur Pardon stood upright in the barge as it emerged from under the bridge on Canal St. Martin. "And we French increasingly have to find jobs overseas. Who knows? Am I destined for a condo in Florida? This is my stop. I live in rue Oberkampf. And you?"

"This will do for me, too." Jerry got ready to disembark. "How long have you lived in Paris?"

"Only for a couple of years. Before that I was a professional autoharp player in Nantes. But the work dried up. I'm currently looking for a job."

They had reached the bank and stood together beside a newspaper kiosk. Jerry took down a copy of *The Herald Tribune* and paid with a three-euro piece.

"You seem lost, m'sieu. Can I help?"

"Thank you. I'm just trying to follow a story. I wonder. May I ask? What makes you cry, M. Pardon?"

The neatly dressed rather serious young man fingered his waxed moustache. He looked down at his pale grey suit, patting his pockets. "Eh?"

"Well, for instance, I cry at almost any example of empathy I encounter. Pretty much any observation of sympathetic imagination. And music. I cry in response to music. Or a generous act. Or a sentimental movie."

M. Pardon smiled. "Well, yes. I am a terrible sentimentalist. I cry, I suppose, when I hear of some evil deed. Or an innocent soul suffering some terrible misfortune."

Jerry nodded, almost to himself. "I understand."

Together, they turned the corner in Rue Oberkampf.

"So it is imagination that moves you to tears?"

"Not exactly. Some forms of imagination merely bore me."

2. SOUTH RAMPART STREET PARADE

Presidential hopeful Rudy Giuliani recently fumbled one of the dumbest questions asked since "boxers or briefs?" Campaigning in Alabama, he was asked, "What is the price of a gallon of milk?" He was off by a buck or two, thus failing a tiresome common-citizen test. But far more important questions need to be posed. Let's start with asking our future leaders about how affordable PCs, broadband

> internet connectivity, and other information technologies are transforming the lives of every American.
>
> —Dan Costa, *PC Magazine*, August 7, 2007

"ANGRY, MR. CORNELIUS?" Miss Brunner unpacked her case. Reluctantly, he had brought her from St. Pancras. Mist was still lifting from St. James's Park. He stood by the window, trying to identify a duck. From this height, it was difficult.

"I'm never angry." He turned as she was hanging a piece of complicated lingerie on a hanger. "You know me."

"A man of action."

"If nothing else." He grew aware of a smell he didn't like. Anaesthetic? Some sort of spray? Was it coming from her case?

"When did you arrive?"

"You met me at Eurostar."

"I meant in Paris. From New Orleans?" That was it. The perfume used to disguise the smell of mould. Her clothes had that specific iridescence. They'd been looted.

"Saks," he said.

"You can't see the label from there, can you? You wouldn't believe how cheap they were."

"*Laissez les bon temps roulez.*" Jerry had begun to cheer up.

"I'm so tired of the English."

3. POMPIER PARIS

> Meet TOPIO.3, the ping-pong playing robot. Made by Vietnam's first ever robotics firm, TOSY the bipedal humanoid uses two 200-fps cameras to detect the ball . . .
>
> —*Popular Science*, March 2010

"HOT ENOUGH FOR YOU? Everyone's leaving for the country." Jerry and Bishop Beesley disembarked from the taxi at the corner of Elgin Crescent and Portobello Road. All the old familiar shops were gone. The pubs had become wine bars and restaurants. Tables and chairs stood outside fake bistros stretching into the middle distance. The fruit and veg on the market stalls had the look of mock organics. Heritage tomatoes. The air was filled with braying aggression. If the heat got any worse there might be a Whiteshirt riot. Jerry could imagine nothing worse than watching the *nouveaux riches* taking it out on what remained of the *anciens pauvres*. The people in the council flats must be getting nervous.

"*Après moi, le frisson nouveau*."

"Do what?" Bishop Beesley was distracted. He had spotted one of his former parishioners stumbling dazedly out of Finch's. The poor bugger had tripped into a timewarp but brightened when he saw the bishop. Sidling up, he mumbled a familiar mantra and forced a handful of old fivers into Beesley's sweating fist. Reluctantly, the bishop took something from under his surplice in exchange. Watching the decrepit speed freak stumble away, he said apologetically, "They're still my flock. But of course there's been a massive falling off compared to the numbers I used to serve. Once, you could rely on an active congregation west of Portobello, but these days everything left is mostly in Kilburn. Not my parish, you see."

Jerry whistled sympathetically.

Beesley stopped to admire one of the newly decorated stalls. The owner, wearing a fresh white overall and a pearly cap, recognized him. "You lost weight, your worship?"

"Sadly . . ." The bishop fingered the stock. "I've never seen brussels as big."

"Bugger me." Jerry stared in astonishment at a fawn bottom rolling towards Colville Terrace. Who needed jodhpurs and green wellies to drive a Range Rover to the Ladbroke Grove Sainsbury's? "Trixie?" Wasn't it Miss Brunner's little girl, all grown up? Distracted, Jerry looked for a hand of long branches that used to hide a sign he remembered on the other side of the Midland Bank. The bank was now an HSBC. Who on earth would want to erase his childhood? He remembered how he used to have a thing against the past. Maybe it was generational.

"Are you okay?" His hand moving restlessly in his pocket, Bishop Beesley looked yearningly across the road at a new sweet and tobacconists called Yummy Puffs. "Would you mind?"

Jerry watched him cross the road and emerge shortly afterwards with his arms full of bags of M&Ms. Where, he wondered absently, were the chocolate bars of yesterday? The Five Boys? He could taste the Fry's peppermint cream on his tongue. Dairy Milk. Those Quakers had known how to make chocolate. As a lad he had wondered why the old Underground vending machines, the Terry's, the Rowntree's, the Cadbury's, were always empty, painted up, like poorly made props meant only to be glimpsed as the backgrounds of Ealing comedies. The heavy cast-iron machines had been sprayed post office red or municipal green, and there was nothing behind the glass panels, no way of opening the sliding dispensers. They had slots for pennies. Signs calling for 2d. They had been empty since the war, he learned from his mum. When chocolate had been rationed and prices had risen. Yet the machines had remained on tube train platforms well into the late 1950s, awaiting new hope; serving to make the Underground mysterious, a tunnel into the past, a labyrinth of memory, where people had once sought sanctuary from bombs. Escalators to heaven and hell. The trains, the ticket machines, the vast escalators, the massive lift cages had all functioned as well as they ever had, but the chocolate machines had become museum pieces, offering a clue to a certain state of mind, a stoicism that perceived them as mere self-indulgence, at odds with the serious business of survival. Not even the most beautiful, desirable machines survived such Puritanism. How many times as a little boy had he hoped that one sharp kick would reward him with an Aero bar, or even a couple of overlooked pennies? And then one day, in the name of modernization, they were carried off, never to be replaced. It was just as well. They had vanished before they could be turned into nostalgic *features*.

Brands meant familiarity and familiarity meant repeated experience and repetition meant security. Once. Now Londoners had achieved the semblance of security, at the very moment when real protection from the fruits of their greed was needed. The Underground had been a false shelter, too, of course. They had poured down there to avoid the bombs, to be drowned and buried. Yet he had loved the atmosphere, the friendship, as he had played with his toy AA gun, his little battery-powered searchlight hunting the dusty arches for a miniature enemy. Portobello began to fill with the yap of *colons* settling their laptops and unfolding their *Independents*, pushing up their sweater sleeves as they sauntered into the pubs, as familiar with their favourite spots as the Germans who had so affectionately occupied Paris.

"They defeated the Underground," Jerry said. "Captured our most potent memories and converted them to cashpoints. They're blowing up everything they don't like. And anything they don't understand, they don't like."

Beesley was looking at him with a certain concern, his lower face pasted with chocolate so that he resembled some Afghan commando. With a plump, dainty finger he dabbed at the corner of his mouth. "Ready?"

Mournfully, Jerry whistled the Marseillaise.

4. LES BOUDINS NOIRS

> Blood-spurting martyrs, biblical parables, ascendant doves—most church windows feature the same preachy images that have awed parishioners for centuries. But a new stained-glass window in Germany's Cologne Cathedral, to be completed in August, evokes technology and science, not religion and the divine.
>
> —*Wired*, August 2007

"ARE YOU FAMILIAR with torture, Herr Cornelius?" Karen von Krupp hitched up her black leather miniskirt and adjusted his blindfold, but over the top he could still see her square, pink face, surrounded by its thick blonde perm, her peachy neck ascending above her swollen breasts. When she reached to pull the mask down he was grateful for the sudden blindness.

"How do you mean 'familiar'?"

"Have you done much of it?"

"It depends a bit on how you define it." He giggled as he heard her crack her little whip. "I used to be able to get into it. Between consenting adults. In more innocent days, you know."

"Oh!" She seemed impatient. Frustrated. "Consent? You mean obedience? Obedient girls?"

Jerry was beginning to understand why he was back in her dentist chair after so many years. "It's Poland all over again, isn't it?"

He heard her light a cigarette, smelled the smoke. A Sullivan's.

She said, "I believe I ask the questions."

"And I respect your beliefs. Did you know that the largest number of immigrants to the U.S. were German? That's why they love Christmas and why they have Easter bunnies, marching bands and think black cats are unlucky." He settled into his bonds. It was going to be a long night.

"Of course. But now I want you to tell me something I don't know."

"I can still see some light."

"We'll soon put a stop to that." Again, she cracked the whip.

"Are we on TV?"

"Should we be?"

"These days, everyone's on TV. Even miners. And riggers. Don't you watch the Guantánamo dailies? Or is it too boring?"

"We don't have cable. Just remember this, Mr. Cornelius. There's more than one way of gassing a canary."

5. LES BOUDINS BLANCS

> The railway from Nairobi to Mombasa is a Victorian relic. But it's the best way to see Kenya.
>
> —*New Statesman*, June 25, 2007

"I GOT THESE rules, see." Shakey Mo looked carefully into the mirror. "That's how I keep on top of things. You can't survive, these days, without rules. Set yourself goals, yeah? Draw up a flow chart. A yearly planner. And then you stick to it. OK? Religiously. Rules is rules. It's survival. It's Mo's survival, anyway." He had begun talking about himself in the third person again. Jerry guessed he was in a bad way.

"Fun?" Jerry stared at the cabinets on the walls. He had to admit Mo kept a neat ship. Each cabinet held a different gun, with its clips, its ammunition, its instruction manual, the date it was acquired, whom it had shot and when.

"Clubbing," Mo told him. "Whenever you get the chance. Blimey, Jerry, where have you been?"

"Rules." Jerry wiped his lovely lips. "The jugged hare seemed a bit bland today. Out of season, maybe? Frozen?"

"There aren't any seasons, these days, Jerry. Just seasoning. Man, you're so retro!" Mo rearranged his hair again. He guffawed. "That's the nineties for you. You need a more fashionable lexicon. You want *au naturel*, you gotta pay for it."

"It wasn't always like this."

"We were young and stupid. We almost lost it. Went too far. That costs, if you're lucky enough to survive. AIDS and the abolition of controlled rents. A high price to pay."

Jerry regarded his shaking hands. "If this is the price of a misspent youth, I'll take a dozen."

Mo wasn't listening. He had found still another reflection. "I think Mo needs a new stylist."

6. HOW TO DEAL WITH A SHRINKING POPULATION

> There's a lot of hot air wafting around the Venice Biennale. But one thing is for sure: the art world can party.
> —*New Statesman*, June 25, 2007

"HI, HI, AMERICAN pie chart." Jerry sniffed. A miasma was creeping across the world. He'd read about it, heard about it, been warned about it. A cloud born of the dreadful dust of conflict, greed, and power addiction, according to old Major Nye. It rose from Auschwitz, London, Hiroshima, Seoul, Jerusalem, Rwanda, New York, and Baghdad. But Jerry wasn't sure. He remarked on it.

Max Pardon buttoned his elegant grey overcoat, nodding emphatically: "*D'accord.*" He resorted to his own language. "We inhale the dust of the dead with every breath. The deeper the breath, the greater the number of others' memories we take to ourselves. Those wind-borne lives bring horror into our hearts, and every dream we have, every anxiety we feel, is a result of all those fires, all those explosions, all those devastations. Out of that miasma shapes are formed. Those shapes achieve substance resembling bone, blood, flesh, and skin, creating monsters, some of them in human form.

"That was how monsters procreated in the heat and destruction of Dachau, the Blitz and the Gaza strip; from massive bombs dropped on the innocent; from massacre and the thick, oily smoke of burning flesh. The miasma accumulated mass as more bombs were dropped and bodies burned. The monsters created from this mass, born of shed blood and human fright, bestrode the ruins of our sanctuaries and savoured our fear like connoisseurs: Here is the Belsen '44; taste the subtle flavours of a Kent State '68 or the nutty sweetness of an Abu Ghraib '05, the amusing lightness of a Madrid '04, a London '06. What good years they were! Perfect conditions. These New York '01s are so much more full-bodied than the Belfast '98s. The monsters sit at table, relishing their feast. They stink of satiation. Their farts expel the sucked-dry husks of human souls: Judge Dredd, Lord Horror, Stuporman. Praise the great miasma wherever it creeps. Into TV sets, computer games, the language of sport, of advertising. The language of politics, infected by the lexicon of war. The language of war wrapped up in the vocabularies of candy-salesmen, toilet sanitizers, room sprays. That filth on our feet isn't dog shit. That city film on our skins is the physical manifestation of human greed. You feel it as soon as you smell New Orleans, Montgomery, or Biloxi.

"That whimpering you heard was the sound of cowards finding it harder and harder to discover sanctuary.

"Where can you hide? The Bahamas? Grand Cayman? The BVAs? The Isle of Man or Monaco? Not now that you've stopped burying treasure, melted the icebergs, called up the tsunamis and made the oceans rise. All that's left is Switzerland with her melting glaciers and strengthened boundaries. The monsters respond by playing dead. This is their moment of weakness when they can be slain, but it takes a special hero to cut off their heads and dispose of their bodies so that they can't rise again. Some Charlemagne, perhaps? Some doomed champion? There can be no sequels. Only remakes. Only remakes. But, because we have exhausted a few of the monsters, that doesn't mean they no longer move amongst us, sampling our souls, watching us scamper in fear at the first signs of their return. We are thoroughly poisoned. We have inhaled the despairing dust of Burundi and Baghdad."

"Well, that was a mouthful." The three of them had crossed the Seine from the Isle St. Louis. It began to get chilly. Jerry pulled on his old car coat and checked his heat. His resurrected needle-gun, primed and charged, was ready to start stitching up the enemy. "Shall we go?"

"You know what my French is like." Mo stared with some curiosity at Max Pardon. A small, neatly wrapped figure wearing an English tweed cap, Pardon had exhausted himself and stood with his back to a gilded statue. "What's he saying?"

"That his taxes are too high," said Jerry.

7. PUMP UP YOUR NETWORK

"*Daran habe ich gar nicht gedacht!*"
—Albert Einstein

"NOW LOOK HERE, Mr. Cornelius, you can't come in here with your insults and your threats. What will happen to the poor beggars who depend on their corps for their healthcare and their massive mortgages? Would you care to have negative equity and be unemployed?" Rupert Fox spread his gnarled antipodean hands, then mournfully fingered the folds of his features, leaning into the mirror-cam. This facelift had not taken as well as he had hoped. He looked like a poorly rehydrated peach. "Platitudes *are* news, old boy." He exposed his expensive teeth to the window overlooking Green Park. In the distance, the six flags of Texas waved all the way up the Mall to Buckingham Palace. "We give them reality in other ways. The reality the public wants. Swelp me. I should know. I've got God. What do you have? A bunch of idols."

"I thought idolatry was your stock in trade."

"Trade makes the world go round."

"The great idolater, eh? All those beads swapped with the natives. All those presents."

"I don't have to listen to this crap." Rupert Fox made a show of good humour. "You enjoy yourself with your fantasies, while I get on with my realities, sport. You can't live in the past forever. Our Empire has to grow and change." He motioned towards his office's outer door. "William will show you to the elevator."

8. IS HE THE GREATEST FANTASY PLAYER OF ALL TIME?

> One of the keys to being seen as a great leader is to be seen as a commander-in-chief . . . My father had all this political capital built up when he drove the Iraqis out of Kuwait and

> he wasted it. If I have a chance to invade . . . if I had that much capital, I'm not going to waste it . . .
>
> —George W. Bush to Mickey Herskowitz, 1999

BANNING NEVER REALLY changed. Jerry parked the Corniche in the disabled parking space and got out. A block to the east, I-10 roared and shook like a disturbed beast. A block to the west, and the town spread to merge with the scrub of semi-desert, its single-storey houses decaying before his eyes. But here, outside Grandma's Kitchen, he knew he was home and dry. He was going to get the best country cooking between Santa Monica and Palm Springs. The restaurant was alone amongst the concessions and chains of Main Street. It might change owners now and again, but never its cooks or waitresses. Never its well-advertised politics, patriotism, and faith. Grandma's was the only place worth eating in a thousand miles. He took off his wide-brimmed Panama and wiped his neck and forehead. It had to be a hundred and ten. The rain, roaring down from Canada and up from the Gulf of Mexico, had not yet reached California. When it did, it would not stop. Somewhere out there, in the heavily irrigated fields, wetbacks were desperately working to bring in the crops before they were swamped. From now on, they would grow rice, like the rest of the country.

Jerry pushed open the door and walked past the display of flags, crosses, fish, and Support Our Troops signs. There was a Christmas theme, too. Every sign and icon had fake snow sprayed over it. Santa and his sleigh and reindeers swung from all available parts of the roof. A big artificial tree in the middle of the main dining room dropped tinsel around its base so that it seemed to be emerging from a sparkling pool. Christmas songs played over the speakers. A few rednecks looked up at him, nodding a greeting. A woman in a red felt elf hat, who might have been the original Grandma, led him through the wealth of red and white chequered table-cloths and wagon-wheel-backed chairs to an empty place in the corner. "How about a nice big glass of ice tea, son?"

"Unsweetened. Thanks, ma'am. I'm waiting for a friend."

"I can recommend the Turkey Special," she said.

Twenty minutes went by before Max Pardon came in, removing his own hat and looking around him in delight. "Jerry! This is perfect. A cultural miracle." The natty Frenchman had shaved his moustache. He had been stationed out here for a couple of months. Banning had once owed a certain prosperity, or at least her existence, to oil. Now she was a dormitory extension for the casinos. You could have bought the whole place for the price of a mid-sized Pasadena apartment. M. Pardon had actually been thinking of doing just that. He ordered his food and gave the waitress one of his sad, charming smiles. She responded by calling him "Darling."

When their meals arrived, he picked up his knife and fork and shrugged. "Don't feel too sorry for me, Jerry. It's healthy enough, once you get back and lose those old interstate habits. You know LA." He spoke idiomatic American. He leaned forward over his turkey dinner to murmur. "I think I've found the guns."

Gladly, Jerry grinned.

As if in response to M. Pardon's information, from somewhere out in the scrubland came the sound of rapid shooting. "That's not the Indians," he said. "The locals do that about this time every day."

"You'll manage to get the guns to the Diné on schedule?"

"Sure." Tasting the fowl, Max raised his eyebrows. "You bet."

Grandma brought them condiments. She turned up her hearing aid, cocking her head. "This'll put Banning on the map." She spoke with cheerful satisfaction. "Just in time to celebrate the season."

Jerry sipped his tea.

Max Pardon always knew how to make the most of Christmas. By the time the Diné arrived, Banning would be a serious bargain.

9. THEY WANT TO MAKE FIREARMS OWNERSHIP A BURDEN – NOT A FREEDOM!

> In August most upscale Parisians head north for Deauville for the polo and the racing or to the cool woods of their country estates in the Loire or Bordeaux . . . Paris's most prestigious hotel at that time of the year is crawling with camera-toting tourists and rubberneckers.
>
> —Tina Brown, *The Diana Chronicles*, 2007

"WELCOME TO THE Hotel California," Jerry sang into his Bluetooth. In his long, dark hair the beautiful violet light winked in time as the ruins sped past on either side of I-10: wounded houses, shops, shacks, filling stations, churches, all covered in dayglo blue PVC, stacks of fallen trunks, piles of reclaimed planks, leaning firehouses, collapsed trees lying where the hurricane had thrown them, overturned cars and trucks, collapsed barns, flattened billboards, flooded strip malls, mountains of torn foliage, state and federal direction signs twisted into tattered scrap, smashed motels and roadside restaurants, mile upon mile of detritus growing more plentiful the closer they got to the coast.

In the identical midnight blue Corniche beside him, connected by her own Bluetooth, Cathy joined in the chorus. The twin cars headed over cypress swamps, bayous and swollen rivers on the way to where the Mississippi met the city.

Standing in the still, swollen ponds on either side of the long bridges, egrets and storks regarded them with cool, incurious eyes. Families of crows hopped along the roadside, pecking at miscellaneous corpses; buzzards cruised overhead. It looked like rain again.

Here and there, massive cracks and gaps in the concrete had been filled in with tar like black holes in a flat grey vacuum. Hand-made signs offered the services of motel chains or burger concessions, and every few miles they were told how much closer they were to Prejean's or Michaux's where the music was still good and the gumbo even tastier. The fish had been enjoying a more varied diet. Zydeco and cajun, crawfish and boudin. Oo-oo. Oo-oo. Still having fon on the bayou . . . Everything still for sale. The Louisiana heritage.

"Them Houston gals done got ma soul!" crooned Cathy. "Nearly home."

10. PIRATES OF THE UNDERSEAS

> At places where two road networks cross, a vertical interchange of bridges and tunnels will separate the traffic systems, and Palestinians from Israelis.
>
> —Eyal Weizman, *Hollow Land: Israel's Architecture of Occupation,* 2007

"CHRISTMAS WON'T BE CHRISTMAS without presents," grumbled Mo, lying on the rug. He got up to sit down again at his keyboard. "Sorry, but that's my experience." He was writing about the authenticity of rules in the game of *Risk.* "I mean you have to give it a chance, don't you? Or you'll never know who you are." He cast an absent-minded glance about the lab. He was in a world of his own.

Miss Brunner came in wearing a white coat. "The kids called. They won't be here until Boxing Day."

"Bugger," said Mo. "Don't they want to finish this bloody game?" He was suspicious. Had her snobbery motivated her to dissuade them, perhaps subtly, from coming? He already had her down as a social climber. Still, a climber was a climber. "Why didn't you let them talk to me?"

"You were out of it," she said. "Or cycling or something. They thought you might be dead."

He shook his head. "There's days I wonder about you."

Catherine Cornelius decided to step in. He was clearly at the end of his rope. "Can I ask a question, Mo?"

Mo took a breath and began to comb his hair. "Be my guest."

"What's this word?" She had been looking at Jerry's notes. "Is this holes, hoes or holds?"

"I think it's ladies," said Mo.

"Oh, of course." She brightened. "Little women. Concord, yes? The dangers of the unexamined life?"

11. REBOOTING THE BODY

> We could hear the Americans counting money and saying to the Pakistanis: "Each person is $5,000. Five persons, $25,000. Seven persons, $35,000."
>
> —Laurel Fletcher and Eric Stover, *The Guantánamo Effect: Exposing the Consequences of U.S. Detention and Interrogation Practices.*

HE HAD BUILT up his identity with the help of toy soldiers, cigarette cards, foreign stamps, all those books from the tuppenny lending library with their wonderful bright jackets preserved in sticky plastic. Netta Muskett was his mum's favourite and he went for P. G. Wodehouse, Edgar Rice Burroughs, P. C. Wren, Baroness Orczy, and the rest. They were still printed in hundreds of thousands then. Thrillers, comedies, fantastic adventure, historical adventure. Rafael Sabatini. What a disappointing picture of him that was in *Lilliput* magazine, wearing waders, holding a rod, caught bending in midstream, an old gent. It came to us all.

Didi Dee seemed to feel more comfortable without her clothes, nodding to herself as she looked at his books. Was she confirming something? He sat in the big Morris library chair and watched her, dark as the mahogany, reflecting the light.

"I wasn't exactly a virgin. My dad started fucking me when I was twelve." She turned to study his reaction. "Does that shock you?"

Jerry laughed. "What? Me? I'm a moralist, I know, but I'm not a petty moralist. You think a spot of finger-wagging is what

Jesus would have done. So I should be saying 'Bloody hell! The fucking bastard'?"

She came back into the bedroom and started snapping on her kit. "It was all right. He got it over with quickly and then he was guilty as hell and I could go out all night and do what and whom I liked without his saying a word because he was scared I'd tell the cops and my mum would find out, though really I think she knew and didn't care. Gave her a quiet life. So by day I was doing my mock A-levels at St. Paul's and by night I was having all the fun of the fair." She blinked reminiscently. "Or thought I was. It took me a bit of time to find out what I liked. What I was like. When I met you I'd just turned twenty-one. I thought I was ready to settle down."

He didn't make the obvious response. He licked the smell of her cunt off his upper lip. He needed a shave. Maybe he'd teach her how to use the straight razor on his face. She required training. She'd said so herself. "What a waste." He thought of those lost nine years.

Suddenly her face opened up into one of those old cheeky grins. A lot better than nothing but it made him want to pee. No, he wasn't really getting that old feeling. She showed him her perfect ass. So this is where nostalgia got you. She lay down next to him. A coquette. "I trust you," she said.

This puzzled him even more. He had once understood her, even if she didn't like him much. Her passivity was her power. It gave her what she wanted or at least it had done so up to now.

He changed the subject a little. "Why are you so cruel to the dead?"

"Because they betrayed me by dying."

"And who will you betray by dying?"

"Who will you betray?"

A no-brainer. "Nobody," he said. "Why?" He suspected one of those boring little traps Christians set for you. Of course God loved him, but he didn't feel very special in this near-infinity of planes that was the multiverse. He was as big as the multiverse, as small as God. It wasn't always this hard to understand.

Space is a dimension of time. Light speed varied enormously. There was a black tide running.

"A black tide running." He tucked her head into his shoulder.

She tensed. "Is that another dig at Obama?"

"What?" He had fallen asleep suddenly. "What about him? Has he betrayed you?"

"That isn't the point. Electing him was what it was about."

"Sure, he's doing such a lot for black pride." Jerry rolled over and found a half-smoked box of Sullivans. He lit one. "God knows what poor old Mandela thinks."

"The Labour Party's trying to find one just like him."

"Hardly worth blacking up for."

From outside came a shout of glee. They both recognized it. Mo was jumping on his prey. He must have caught a kid.

12. POPSCI'S GUIDE TO SUMMER SCI-TECH MOVIES

> Staring at the vast military history section of the airport shop, I had a choice: the derring-do of psychopaths or scholarly tomes with their illicit devotion to the cult of organized killing. There was nothing I recognized from reporting war. Nothing on the spectacle of children's limbs hanging in trees and nothing on the burden of shit in your trousers. War is a good read. War is fun. More war, please.
>
> —John Pilger, *New Statesman*, May 10, 2010

MO WASN'T HAVING any and neither, he remarked happily, had he been getting any. But there was this little yellow lady to the west of Kathmandu and the crew had come to know her just as "Belle." They were banging on the wedding gongs and decorating dresses, and they were praying that she didn't go to hell, because Mo he was a white man and not the best at that and they didn't want their girl to wear his band. They consoled themselves, however, that they needn't curse the moon for poor Belle would be a widow pretty soon. So they smiled at Mo and offered him the best seat in the house until Belle herself, she said, could smell a rat. And they put their heads together and they made a little plan to see her married by some other means or man. Really, Mo thought, he was probably a goner.

"Mo?"

He turned. He had been on his feet long enough to understand his bit as he fell onto the carpet. Buggered.

He could still hear. "Of course it's not curare."

Jerry was wistful as he watched Mitzi Beesley drag the little fellow into the hedge. "But then again it's not chocolate, either!"

"I wouldn't personally be talking about sweets," Didi Dee murmured. She had become shy. Flirtatious. Weak. Self-righteous. Religious.

Why was she searching out his contempt?

This whole thing was altogether too retro for Jerry. He cleared his throat, spat on the ground. Where was his 1954? Surely earlier? What numbers had she offered him?

Should he get into the spirit of the times? Feeling guilty. Finding places to hide. Telling lies? You needed a voice. He couldn't muster a voice on top of everything else.

Somewhere up there in the diminishing hills he heard an engine. Jimmy van Dorn's awful old Rolls-Royce.

Time to be shunting along. He kissed Didi on her dimpled cheek. "Tee tee eff en."

THE WHEELS OF CHANCE

1. GUNS IS GUNS

Everyone will be wealthy, living like a lord,
Getting plenty of things today they can't afford
But when's it going to happen? When? Just by and by!
Oh, everything will be lovely, when the pigs begin to fly!
—Charles Lambourne, *Everything Will Be Lovely*, c. 1860

During the tour you will visit many of the key sites connected to these infamous "Whitechapel Murders." You will retrace the footsteps of Jack The Ripper and discover, when, where and how his five unfortunate victims lived and died. You will also discover why the Ripper was never caught and what life was really like for people living in the London's notorious East End.

FREE Jack The Ripper starts and finishes at Mary Jane's, named after the Ripper's fifth and final victim, Mary Jane Kelly, where from 6pm you have access to 2-4-1 house cocktails, 2-4-1 bottles of Kronenbourg, £8.90 bottles of house wine, £8.90 cocktail jugs and 3-4-2 on all small plates of food . . . what a killer offer!!!
—*Celebrity & Pop Culture Tours of the Planet*, Celebrity Planet 2010

"I ADMIRE A MAN who can look cool on a camel." Bessy Burroughs presented Jerry with her perfectly rounded vowels. Born in Kansas, she had been educated in Sussex, near Brighton. Regular vowels, her dad had always said, were the key to success, no matter what your calling. "God! Is it always this hot in Cairo?"

"It used to be lovely in the winter." Jerry jumped down from his kneeling beast and came to help Bessy dismount. Only Karen von Krupp preferred to remain in her saddle. Shielding her eyes against the rising sun, she peered disdainfully at a distant clump of palms.

Bessy had none of her father Bunny's lean, lunatic wit. Her full name was Timobeth, a combination of those her parents had chosen for a girl or a boy. Bunny believed that old-fashioned names were an insult to the future. They pandered to history. Her parents still hated history. A sense of the past was but a step on the road to nostalgia and nostalgia, as Bunny was fond of saying, was a vice that corrupts and distorts.

Jerry remembered his lazy lunches at Rules. Bunny had loved Rules. But he had come to hate the heritage industry as "a brothel disguised as a church." Jerry wasn't sure what he meant and had never had a chance to find out. If he turned up, as promised, by the Sphinx, perhaps this would be a good time to ask him.

"Dad loves it out here." Pulling her veil from her hat to her face, Bessy began to follow him across the hard sand towards the big pyramid. "Apart from the old stuff. He hates the old stuff. But he loves the beach. The old stuff can crumble to dust for all he cares." She paused to wipe her massive cheeks and forehead. That last box of Turkish delight was beginning to tell on her. She had been raised, by some trick of fate, by Bishop Beesley as his own daughter until Mitzi had finally objected and Bunny had been recalled from Tangier to perform his paternal duties.

"You don't like to be connected to the past?" asked Karen von Krupp, bringing up a lascivious leer and with a curious-looking whip thwacking her "Charlie" on its rump. "I love history. So romantic."

"Hate it. Loathe it. History disgusts me. Hello! Who's this type, I wonder?"

"Good god!" Suddenly fully awake, Jerry pushed back his hat. "Talk about history! It's Major Nye."

Major Nye, in the full uniform of Skinner's Horse, rode up at a clip and brought his grey to a skidding stop in the sand.

"Morning, major."

"Morning, Cornelius. Where's that hotel gone?"

"I gather it had its day, major. Demolished. I can't imagine what's going up in its place." His knees were cramping.

"I can." With a complacent hand, Bessy patted a brochure she produced from a saddlebag. "It's going to be like The Pyramid. That's why I asked you all here. Only three times bigger. And in two buildings. You'll be able to get up in the morning and look down on all that." She waved vaguely in the direction of the pyramids. "It'll be a knockout. It will knock you *unconscious*! Really!" She nodded vigorously, inviting them, by her example, to smile. "It did me. I daren't ask what diverting the Nile's going to cost. But it's guaranteed terrorist free."

"Gosh," said Jerry. Major Nye peered gravely down at his horse's mane.

"We are born unconscious and we die unconscious." Karen von Krupp gestured with her whip. "In between we suffer precisely because we are conscious, whereas the other creatures with whom we share this unhappy planet are unconscious forever, no? I was not. I am. I shall not be. Is this the past, present and future? Is this what we desire from Time?"

"Rather." Bessy nodded for good luck, approval and physical power. All the things deprived her in her childhood. Massive tears of self-pity ran rhythmically down her face. "This heat! These allergies!"

"I must apologize, dear lady. I'm not following you, I fear."

"This hotel I'm talking about. Two big pyramids. Sheraton are interested already."

"Ah, but the security." Karen von Krupp laid her whip against her beautiful leg and arranged her pleated skirt. "These days. What can you guarantee?"

"No problem. Indonesians. Germans. French. British. The cream of the crop."

"I prefer Nubians," said Jerry.

"These will be as stated. No Saudis or Pashtoon, either. That's non-negotiable."

Jerry looked up. From the far horizon came the steady thump of helicopter engines, then the sharper thwacking of their blades. He had a feeling about this. "Nubians or nothing," he said. And began to run back towards his camel.

Almost at ground level, rising and falling with the dunes, eight engines roaring in a terrible, shrill chorus, the massive, two-tiered monster of mankind's miserable imagination, the Dornier DoX flying boat appeared over the oasis and attempted to land on the brackish water from which their camels were now shying. Their clothing and harnesses were whipped by the wind from its propellers. As soon as she had made a pass or two over the watering hole and failed, the Dornier lumbered up into the air and out of sight, still seeking to complete the round-the-world-flight she had begun to break when she set out from the Bavarian lakes four and a half years ago.

"What I can't work out," said Jerry, "is how it took them so long to get the power-weight ratio right."

He cocked his head, listening for the plane's return.

"I wonder who's flying her this evening."

2. THE BRANDY AND SELTZER BOYS

> According to quantum theory, a card perfectly balanced on its edge will fall down in what is known as a "superposition"—the card really is in two places at once. If a gambler bets money on the queen landing face up, the gambler's own state changes to become a superposition of two possible outcomes—winning or losing the bet in either of these parallel worlds, the gambler is unaware of the other outcome and feels as if the card fell randomly.
>
> —*Nature,* July 5, 2007

"WE NEED RITUALS, Jerry. We need repetition. We need music and mythology and the constant reassurance that at certain times of the day we can visit the waterhole in safety. Without ritual, we are worthless. That's what the torturer knows when he takes away even the consistent repetition of our torment."

Bunny Burroughs ordered another beer. There were still a few minutes to Curtain Up. This was to be the first time Gloria Cornish and Una Persson had appeared on the same stage. A revival. *The Arcadians.*

"These are on me." Jerry signed for the bill. "Repetition is a kind of death. It's what hopeless people do—what loonies do—sitting and rocking and muttering the same meaningless mantras over and over again. That's not conscious life."

"We don't *want* conscious life." Miss Brunner, coming in late, gave her coat to Bishop Beesley to take to the cloakroom. "Have I got time for a quick G&T? We don't want real variety. From the catchphrase of the comedian to the reiteration of familiar opinions, they're the beating of a mother's heart, the breathing of a sleeping father."

"Maybe we've at last dispossessed ourselves of the past. We name our children after bathroom products, fantasy characters, drugs, diseases, and candy bars. We used to name them after saints or popular politicians . . ." Jerry finished his beer. A bell began to ring.

"That's just a different kind of continuity. The trusted brand has taken over from the trusted saint." Miss B picked up her program. "We're still desperate for the familiar. We try to discard it in favour of novelty, but it isn't really novelty, it's just another kind of familiarity. We tell ourselves of our self-expression and self-assertion. When I was a girl, my days were counted in terms of food. Sunday was a hot joint. Tuesday was cold sliced meat, potatoes and a vegetable. Wednesday was shepherd's pie. Thursday was cauliflower cheese. Friday was fish. Saturday, we had a mixed grill. With chips. Just as lessons came and went at school, we attended the Saturday matinee, Sunday at a museum. Something uplifting, anyway, on Sunday. We move forward by means of rituals. We just try to find the means of keeping the carousel turning. We sing work songs as we build roads. Music allows a semblance of progression, but it isn't real progression. Real progress leads where? To the grave, if we're lucky? Our stories are the same, with minor variations. We're comfortable, with minor variations, in the same clothes. The sun comes up and sets at the same time and we welcome the rise and fall of the workman's hammer, the beat of the drum. If we really wanted to cut our ties with the past we would do the only logical thing. We would kill ourselves."

"Isn't that just as boring?"

"Oh, I guess so, Mr. Cornelius." Bunny petted at his face and put down his empty glass.

As they walked towards their box, the overture was striking up.

3. FROM CLUE TO CLUE

> The theme of the Wandering Jew has a history of centuries behind it, and many are the romances which that sinister and melancholy figure has flitted through. In this story you will see how the coming of the mythical Wanderer was a direct threat to the existence of our Empire, and how, when he, as the figurehead of revolt faded out of the picture, Sexton Blake tackled the real causes behind it.
>
> —"The Case of the Wandering Jew," *Sexton Blake Annual*, 1940

"I'M RUNNING OUT of memory." Jerry put his head on one side, like a parrot. "Or at best storage. I'm forgetting things. I think I might have something."

"Oh, god, don't give it to us." Miss Brunner became contemplative. "Is it catching? Like Alzheimer's?"

"I don't remember." Jerry took an A to Z from the pocket of his black car coat. "It depends whether it's the past or the present. Or the future. I remember where Berwick Street is in Soho and I could locate Decatur Street. I'm not losing my bearings any worse than usual. Why is everyone trying to forget?"

"It wasn't part of the plan. I'm a bit new to this." Bunny Burroughs glanced hopefully at Miss Brunner. "I think."

Now Jerry really was baffled. "Plan?"

"The plan for America. Remember Reagan?"

"Vaguely," said Jerry. He pointed ahead of him. "If that's not a mirage, we've found an oasis."

"He's all turned around, poor thing," said Miss von Krupp.

4. THE NEW XJ – LUXURY TRANSFORMED BY DESIGN

> Freighter captains avoid them as potential catastrophes, climate scientists see them as a bellwether of global warming. But now marine biologists have a more positive take on the thousands of icebergs that have broken free from Antarctica in recent years. These frigid, starkly beautiful mountains of floating ice turn out to be bubbling hot spots of biological activity. And in theory at least they could help counteract the buildup of greenhouse gases that are heating the planet.
>
> —Michael D. Lemonick, *Time* magazine, August 6, 2007

"THEY'VE BEEN IN Trinity churchyard digging up the famous. I can't tell you how much they got for Audubon." Jerry sipped his chicory and coffee. The Café du Monde wasn't what it had been but they'd taken the worst of the rust off the chairs, and the joss sticks helped. From somewhere down by the river came the broken sound of a riverboat bell. Then he began to smile at his friend across the table. "That was you, wasn't it?"

Max Pardon shrugged. "We were downsized. What can I say? We have to make a living as best we can. The bottom dropped out of real estate. I'm a bone broker, these days, Mr. Cornelius. It's an honest job. Some of us still have an interest in our heritage. Monsieur Audubon was a very great man. He made his living, you could say, as a resurrectionist. Mostly. He killed that poor, mad, golden eagle. Do I do anything worse?"

Jerry took a deep breath and regretted it.

The oil had not proved the blessing some had predicted.

5. THE FLOODS THAT REALLY MATTER ARE COMPOSED OF MIGRANT LABOUR

> Intimate talk about loving your age, finding true joy. and the three words that can change your life.
>
> —*Good Housekeeping,* June 2005

IN ISLAMABAD, JERRY traded his Banning for an antique Lee-Enfield 303 with a telescopic sight. He had come all the way by aerial cruiser, the guest of Major Nye, with the intention of seeing, if he could do it secretly, his natural son Hussein, who was almost ten. Slipping the beautifully embellished rifle into his cricket bag, he made for an address on Kabul Street, ridding himself of two sets of "shadows." The most recent Islamic government was highly suspicious of all Europeans, even though Jerry's Turkish passport gave his religion as Moslem. He wore a beautifully cut coat in two shades of light blue silk, with a set of silver buttons and a turban in darker blue. To the casual eye he resembled a prosperous young stockbroker, perhaps from Singapore.

Arriving at Number Eight, Jerry made his way through a beautiful courtyard to a shaded staircase, which he climbed rapidly after a glance behind him to see if he was followed. On the third floor about halfway down the landing he stopped and knocked. Almost immediately the recently painted door was opened and Bunny Burroughs let him in, his thin lips twisting as he recognized the cricket bag.

"Your fifth attempt, I understand, Jerry. Did you have a safe trip? And will you be playing your usual game this Sunday?"

"If I can find some whites." Jerry set the bag down and removed his rifle. With his silk handkerchief he dabbed at his sleeve. "Oil. Virgin. Is the boy over there?"

"With his nanny. The mother, as I told you, is visiting her uncle."

Jerry peered through the slats of a blind. Across the courtyard, at a tall window, a young woman in a sari was mixing a glass of diluted lemon juice and sugar. Behind her the blue screen of a TV was showing an old Humphrey Bogart movie.

"*Casablanca*," murmured Bunny.

"*The Big Sleep*." Jerry lifted the rifle to his shoulder and put his eye close to the sight.

He would never know another sound like that which followed his pulling of the trigger and the bang the gun made.

He had done the best he could. That at least he understood.

Was that a mosquito? He slapped his face.

6. THE PHANTOM OF THE TOWERS

> International trade in great white sharks now will be regulated, which is especially important for fish who range far beyond the shelter of regional protection. The humphead or Napoleon wrasse—worth tens of thousands of dollars on the market—also received protections, in turn saving coral reefs from the cyanide used to capture them.
>
> —*Animal Update*, Winter 2005

HUBERT LANE AND Violet Elizabeth Bott were waiting on the corner for Jerry as soon as he reached the outskirts of the village. He had driven over from Hadley to see old Mr. Brown. Hubert smirked when he saw Jerry's Phantom IV. "You've done a lot better for yourself than anyone would have guessed a few years ago."

Jerry ignored him.

"Hewwo, Jewwy," lisped Violet Elizabeth, rather grotesquely coy for her age. "Wovely to see you."

Jerry scowled. He was already regretting his decision but he opened the gate and began to walk up the surprisingly overgrown path. The Browns clearly hadn't kept their gardener on. Things had deteriorated rather a lot since 1978. The front door of the double fronted Tudor-style detached house could do with a lick of paint. The brass needed a polish, too. He lifted the knocker.

The door was opened by a woman in uniform.

"Mr. 'Cornelius'?"

"That's right."

"Mr. Brown said you were coming. He's upstairs. I'm the District Nurse. I hung on specially. This way."

She moved her full lips in a thin, professional smile and took him straight upstairs. The house smelled familiar and the wallpaper hadn't changed since his last visit. Mrs. Brown had been alive then. The older children, Ethel and Robert, had been home from America and Australia respectively.

"They're expected any time," said the nurse when he asked. She opened the bedroom door. Now the medicinal smell overwhelmed everything else. Old Mr. Brown was completely bald. His face was much thinner. Jerry no longer had any idea of his age. He looked a hundred.

"Hello, boy." Mr. Brown's voice was surprisingly vibrant. "Nice of you to drop in." His smile broadened. "Hoping for a tip, were you?"

"Crumbs!" said Jerry.

7. A GAME OF PATIENCE

> The new centre-right government in UK unveiled on Tuesday the first of its series of measures to curb immigration, saying Indians must now pass English tests if they wanted to marry a British citizen.
>
> —*The Times of India*, June 9, 2010

BANNING BEHIND HIM, Mo put the Humvee in gear and set off across a desert which reminded him of Marilyn Monroe, Charles Manson and Clark Gable. Tumbleweed, red dust, the occasional cactus, yucca, jasper trees. He was heading west and south, trying to avoid the highways. Eventually he saw mountains.

A couple of days later, he woke Jerry who had been asleep in the back since Banning.

"Here we are, Mr. C."

Jerry stretched out on the old rug covering the floor of the vehicle. "Christmas should be Christmas now we've presents." He blinked out of the window at a butte. There were faces in every rock. This was the Southwest as he preferred it.

Mo was dragging his gun behind him as he squeezed into a narrow fissure, one of several in the massive rockface. According to legend, a hunted Indian army had made this its last retreat. Somewhere within, there was water, grass, even corn. The countless variegated shades of red and brown offered some hint of logic, at least symmetry, swirling across the outcrops and natural walls as if painted by a New York expressionist. They reminded Jerry of those ochre Barsoomian Dead Sea bottoms he had loved in his youth. He had been born in London, but he had been raised on Mars. He could imagine the steady movement of waves overhead. He looked up.

Zuni knifewings had been carved at intervals around the entrance of the canyon; between each pair was a swastika.

"I wonder what they had against the Jews," said Mo. He paused to take a swig from his canteen.

Jerry shrugged. "You'd have thought there was a lot in common."

Now Mo disappeared into the fissure. His voice echoed. "It's huge in here. Amazing. I'll start placing the charges, shall I?"

Jerry began to have second thoughts. "This doesn't feel like Christmas anymore."

Behind them, on the horizon, a Diné or Apaché warband sat on ponies so still they might have been carved from the same ancient rock.

Jerry sighed. "Or bloody Kansas!" He started to set up his Banning. He was getting tired of this. It had turned out to be much harder work than they'd suggested.

8. A CITY SLICKER EMAILED IN THE STICKS

> Tony Blair claims that one of his many achievements in office was not to repeal the employment laws passed by Margaret Thatcher's government to weaken trade union power. But Blair, as a young and politically ambitious barrister, was a staunch supporter of trade union rights.
>
> —*New Statesman*, June 25, 2007

"I KNOW WHERE you're coming from, Jerry." Bunny Burroughs closed his laptop. Of course he didn't. He had only the vaguest idea. Jerry didn't even bother to tell him about *The Magnet*, Sexton Blake or George Formby. They certainly had some memories in common, but even those were filtered through a mix of singular cultural references that changed the simplest meaning. Bunny's baseball and Cornelius's cricket: the list was endless. Yet somehow exile brought out the best in them. They would always have Paris.

Jerry sniffed. "Are you still selling that stuff?"

"Virtual vapour? It's very popular. While thousands die in Rwanda, millions watch TV and concern themselves with the fate of the mountain gorilla whose time in the world is actually less limited. Assuming zoos continue to do their stuff." He held up a can. "Want a sniff?" He peered round at the others. "Anybody?"

"If I had a shilling for every year I've thought about the future, I'd be a rich man today." Bishop Beesley hesitated before slipping a Heath Bar between his lips and breathing in the soft scent of chocolate and burned sugar. "Sweet!" He let a sentimental smile drift across his lips. "I know it's a weakness, but which of us isn't weak somewhere? I live to forget. I mean forgive. I've a parish in South London now. Did you know?"

"I think you told me."

"No," said Bill.

"No? It's only across the river. We could."

"No." Jerry continued to look for a channel. "I don't cross running water if I can help it. And I don't do snow."

"It's really not as cold as people say it is. Even Norbury's warmer than you'd guess. Kingsley Amis grew up there. And Edwy Searles Brooks. Brooks was the most famous person to come from Norbury. St. Franks? Waldo the Wonderman? And Frank Bellamy. You know. In *The Eagle.* Not to mention rock and roll. Martin Stone, England's greatest electric guitarist—"

Jerry shuddered. He'd be hearing about the wonders of Wimbledon next. Tactfully he asked if Beesley knew a second-hand tire shop easily reached.

"There's even a beach of sorts." The bishop breathed impatience. "Where Tooting Common used to be. The water's invigorating, I'm told. Though they haven't axed the chestnut trees."

"They must be borders," suggested Bill.

"Still plenty for the little 'uns."

"Plenty?"

"Conkers." The bishop put a knowing hand on Jerry's arm. "Don't worry. No ward of mine has ever come to harm."

"Conkers? No, you're barmy. Bonkers." Jerry shook him off, swiftly walking to the outside door.

"Pop in. Anytime. You've not forgotten how to pray?" The bishop's voice was muffled, full of half-masticated Heath.

Jerry paused, trying to think of a retort.

Bunny Burroughs stood up, his thin body awkward beneath the cloth of his loose, charcoal grey suit. "I am a gloomy man, Mr. Cornelius. I have a vision. Follow me. Of the appalling filth of this world, I am frequently unobservant. Once I revelled in it, you could fairly say. Now it disgusts me. I am no longer a lover of shit. I came on the streetcar. That's what I like about Europe, the streetcars. Environment-friendly and everything. They have a narrative value you don't run into much any more. Certainly not in America. My mother was German. Studied eugenics, I think. On the evidence. But I'm English on my father's side. I fought on my father's side."

He turned to look out of the window. "The slaveships threw over the dead and dying. Typhoon coming on." He picked up the laptop. "Trained octopi drove those trams, they say."

Jerry said, "OK. I give up. When can you get me connected?"

"It depends." Burroughs frowned, either making a calculation or pretending to make one. "It depends how much memory you want. Four to seven days?" His long, sad face contemplated some invisible chart. His thin fingers played air computer. "Any options?"

Jerry had become impatient. "Only connect," he said. God, how he yearned for a taste of the real world. The world he had been sure he knew. Even Norbury.

The old trees they knew as the Manor grew in ground surrounding the Barclay's Bank and were more or less public until the cricket club became more conscious of its privacy. The egalitarian spirit disappeared rapidly with the success of the first postwar Conservative government.

The best woods lay on top of Biggin Hill where one of wartime Britain's most active airfields had lain in the flat delta where two valleys met. Croydon had been another. Then Norbury Cross, carved out of Mitcham Common and restored, when Jerry first went back, to a replica of its prewar appearance.

It didn't do to get sentimental. Jerry felt cold again. His breath was thick on the rapidly cooling air. But he had spent too many years finding this place to risk losing it completely.

High elms where the rooks nested making the sharpness of an autumn evening, the smell of woodsmoke, the red and orange skies on the horizon, the noise of the returning birds. Like laughter. Sneering, quarrelsome laughter.

Once real wealth came into the equation, the seeds of fresh class warfare were sewn as the salaries grew farther apart and bonuses became a kind of Danegeld to dissuade directors from taking their strength elsewhere. Most of that strength lay in guilty secrets.

"What the bloody hell do ya think you're doing sitting there dreaming, ya silly-looking toad! Go and get us some fish and chips."

"Yes, mum." He climbed out of the sheet under which

he'd been hiding to frighten his brother Frank.

"Can you smell pee?" she asked anxiously as he went out through the front door. "Tell me if ya can smell it when ya come in, love."

9. THE MOST FUEL-EFFICIENT AUTO COMPANY IN AMERICA

> BRUSSELS: A Belgian high school today sacked a Muslim maths teacher after she insisted she would continue to wear the burqa while taking classes.
>
> —*The Times of India,* June 9, 2010

"WHAT I CAN'T understand about you, Mr. Cornelius," Miss Brunner said, opening a cornflower blue sunshade only slightly wider than her royal blue Gainsborough hat, "is why so many of your mentors are gay. Or Catholic. Or both."

"Or Jewish," said Jerry. "You can't forget the Jews. It's probably the guilt."

"You? Guilt? Have you ever felt guilt?"

"That's not the point." He found himself thinking again of Alexander, his unborn son. Invisibly, he collected himself. "I reflect it."

"That's gilt. Not guilt."

"Oh, believe me. They're often the same thing."

From somewhere beyond the crowd a gun cracked.

She brightened, quickening her high-heeled trot. "They're off!"

Jerry tripped behind her. There was something about Surrey he was never going to like.

10. THE SLEEP YOU'VE BEEN DREAMING OF

> The creator of the Segway is one of the most successful and admired inventors in the world. He leads a team of 300 scientists and engineers devoted to making things that better mankind. But Dean Kamen won't feel satisfied until he achieves his greatest goal: reinventing us.
>
> —*Popular Mechanics*, June 2010

BACK IN ISLAMABAD Jerry read the news from New Orleans. He wondered if the French were going to regret their decision to buy it back. How could they possibly make it pay? The cleanup alone had already bankrupted BP. It hadn't been a great couple of years for the oligarchs. Of course, it did give France the refineries and a means of getting their tankers up to Memphis, but how would the American public take to the reintroduction of the minstrels on the showboats?

"People who are free, who live in a real republic, are never offended, Jerry. At best they are a little irritated. They should be able to take a joke by now. In context."

"Wait till they burn *your* bloody car." Jerry was still upset about what had happened in Marseilles.

"They are citizens. They have the same rights and responsibilities as me." Max Pardon swung his legs on his stool. He had rewaxed his moustache. Possibly with cocoa butter.

Jerry lit a long, black Sherman. "At least you've brought back smoking."

"That's the Republic, Jerry."

Max Pardon raised his hat to a passing Bedouin. "God bless the man who discovered sand-power." Overhead the last of the great aerial steamers made its stately way into the sunrise just as the muezzin began to call the faithful to prayer. Monsieur Pardon unrolled his mat and kneeled. "If you'll forgive me."

11. WHY I LOVE METAL

> It's what you've been craving. Peaceful sleep without a struggle. That's what LUNESTA© is all about: helping most people fall asleep quickly, and stay asleep all through the night. It's not only non-narcotic; it's approved for long-term use.
>
> —Ad for Eszopiclone in *Time* magazine, August 6, 2007

"I AM SICK of people who can't distinguish the taste of sugar from the taste of fruit, who can't tell salt from cheese, who think watching CNN makes them into intellectuals and believe that *Big Brother* and *The Bachelor* are real life. The richest, most powerful country in the world is about as removed from reality as Oz is from Kansas or Kansas is from Kabul or Obama is from Kenya." Major Nye was in a rare mood as he leaned over the rail of *The Empress of India* searching with his binoculars for his old station. His long, ancient fingers with their thin tanned skin resembled the claws of an albino crow he had once kept at the station. "Which half knows Africa best? Bleeding Africa . . ."

From somewhere among the bleak rolling downs, puffs of smoke showed the positions of the Pashtoon.

"I remember all the times the British tried to invade and hold Afghanistan. What surprises me is why these Yanks think they are somehow better at it, when they've never won a war by themselves since the Mexicans decided to let them have California. Every few years they start another bloody campaign and refuse to listen to their own military chaps and go swaggering in to get their bottoms kicked for the umpteenth time. Then they turn on the French and the Italians whom they consider inferior warriors to themselves. The Europeans learned their lessons. They knew how easy it was to start a war and how difficult it was to finish one. The Americans learned an unfortunate lesson from their successes against the Indians, such as they were. If you ask me, they would have done better to have taken a leaf from Custer's book."

"Education's never been their strength." Holding her hat with her left hand, Miss Brunner waved and smiled at someone in the observation gallery. "It's windy out here, don't you think?"

"Better than that fug in there." Major Nye indicated the Smoking Room. With a gesture close to impatience, he threw his cigarette over the side.

As if in answer, another rifle-shot echoed below.

Miss Brunner looked down disapprovingly. "There should be more public shootings, if you ask me. Why are the decent ones always the first to be taken? They should just be more selective." She looked up, directing a frigid smile at Mitzi Beesley, who came out to join them. Mitzi was wearing a borrowed flying helmet, a short, pink divided skirt, a flounced white blouse, a knitted bolero jacket.

Mitzi was going through her radical phase. "That's exactly what the YCFA says. You pinched that from the Left."

"Oh, we pinched a lot from the Left. Just as the Right pinched from us. When the Left have become Centre Right and the Right has become reactionary, you know exactly where you stand, eh? Exactly. How many times in the last century did you see that?" Miss Brunner laughed happily. "Oh, I do love old times, don't you? And the one-party system."

Jerry remembered her closing the gate of her Hampstead Garden Village bijou cottage, as she left him in charge for a week. That had been the last time they had met. She was no longer speaking to him. He went back into the bar and closed the door. It seemed almost silent here; just the soft hum of the giant electric motors. He accepted a pint of Black Velvet. He had a rat buttoned inside his coat. Its nose tickled his chest and he gave an involuntary twitch. Mitzi still didn't know he had rescued "Sweety" from the fire. He had grown attached to the little animal and felt Mitzi was an imperfect owner.

The Bengali barman polished a glass. "Life's a bloody tragedy, isn't it sir? Same again?"

Outside, the rain began to drum on the canopy. Major Nye and the women came running in. "I for one will be glad to get back to Casablanca," said Miss Brunner.

12. OBAMA, BARBOUR MEET ON COAST

> Until recently, criticisms of the BBC were helpful, and attacks upon it harmless, indeed it provided, among other blessings, a happy grumbling ground for the sedentary, where they could release their superfluous force . . . and if not much good was done there was anyhow no harm . . . Unfortunately, (the BBC's) dignity is only superficial. It does yield to criticism, and to bad criticism, and it yields in advance—the most pernicious of surrenders.
>
> —E. M. Forster, *New Statesman,* April 4, 1931

JERRY HAD SHOWERED and was putting on his regular clothes when Professor Hira came into the changing rooms.

"You were superb today, Mr. Cornelius. Especially under the circumstances."

Jerry accepted his handshake. "Oh, you know, it's not as if they got the whole of London."

"Hampstead, Islington, Camden! The Heath is a pit of ash. We saw the cloud on TV. Red and black. The blood! The smoke. Of course, we know that our bombs, for instance, are much more powerful. But Hampstead Garden Village! My home was there for over four years. The Beesleys, too. And so many other dear neighbours."

"You think it was their target?"

"No doubt about it. And next time it will be Hyde Park or Wimbledon Common. Even Victoria Park. They are easy to home in on, you see."

"Another park is where they'll strike next?"

"Or, heaven forbid, Lords. Or the Oval."

"Good god. They'll keep the ashes forever!"

"Our fear exactly." Professor Hira took Jerry's other hand. "You plan, I hope, to stay in Mombai for a bit? We could do with a good all-rounder."

Jerry considered this. It was quite a while since he'd been to the pictures. "It depends what's on, I suppose." He bent and picked up his cricket bag. "And I'm sure it's still possible to get a game or two in before things become too hot."

"Oh, at least. And, Mr. Cornelius, it will never be too hot for you in India. Pakistan has far too many distractions, what with the Americans and their own religeuses."

Jerry scratched his head. Reluctant as he was to leave, he thought it was time he got back home again.

13. THE TEARS I SHARED WITH LAURA BUSH

> The most ambitious weapons program in Army history calls for a whole new arsenal of connected gear, from helicopter drones to GPS-guided missiles. But what happens if the network that links it all isn't ready?
>
> —*Popular Science*, May 2009

THE BATS WERE rising over Austin as usual. Mo had at last given up trying to count them and was eating a hot dog. He was resentful. He had been told that Texas was the most gun-friendly state in the Union, but had been stopped four times from carrying his Banning into the Capitol. "Fucking hypocrites."

"Sir, I must really ask you again to watch your language."

Mo recognized the Texas Ranger. Jerry caught him in time. The bats rose in a long, lazy curve against the dark blue evening sky. It was time to get back to the desert. Jerry had had enough of culture.

He had only come here to get himself a real cowboy hat.

He explained this to the Ranger. "I suppose you couldn't sell me yours? I think we're about the same head size."

But he hadn't distracted the Ranger long enough.

"Were you fucking talking to me?" Mo came gleefully forward.

Jerry sighed. He had a feeling they weren't going to be leaving as quietly as he'd hoped. He took out his mobile and dialled Didi Dee. He hated to cancel dinner so close to the time.

He looked at his wrists.

"What's the time? My watches have stopped."

14. BETRAYAL IN IRAQ

> **MEN LOVE POWER.** Why? Ever see what happens when something gets in the way of a tornado? Exactly. That's the thinking behind the Chevy Vortec™ Max powertrain—create a ferocious vortex inside the combustion chamber, along with a high compression ratio, to generate formidable power. And the 345-hp Vortec™ Max, available on the 2006 Silverado, is no exception . . . **CHEVY SILVERADO: AN AMERICAN REVOLUTION.**
>
> —Chevrolet ad, *Texas Monthly*, December 2005

CHRISTMAS 1962. SNOW was still falling just after dawn when Jerry sprung the gate into Ladbroke Grove/Elgin Gardens and walked onto the path, leaving black pointed prints and tiny heel marks. He had never made a cooler trail. Slipping between the gaps in the netting, he crossed the tennis court and stopped to look back. The marks might have been those of an exotic animal. Nobody coming behind him would know a human had made them. Yet they were already filling up again.

He would never be sure he had deceived anyone. He darted into the nearest back garden. From the French windows came the sound of a Schoenberg piano roll. The snow was a foot deep against the brick wall, on the small lawn. Yellow light fell from the window above. He heard a woman's voice not unlike his mother's. "Go back to bed, love. It's not time yet." He recognized Mrs. Pash. Her grandchildren were up early, pedalling the piano. He caught a glimpse of the tree through the half-drawn curtains.

Jerry stepped softly out of the little garden. A blind moved on the first floor in the corner house. The colonel and his wife were looking at him. Another minute and they'd call the police. Their hangovers always made them doubly suspicious. He bowed and went back the way he had come, back into Ladbroke Grove, back across to Blenheim Crescent, past the Convent of the Poor Clares, on his left, to 51, where his mother still lived.

Humming to himself, Jerry went down the slippery area steps to let himself in with his key. Nobody was up. He unshipped the sack from his shoulder and checked out the row of stockings hanging over the black, greasy kitchen range from which a few wisps of smoke escaped. He opened the stove's top and shovelled in more coke. His mum had put the turkey in to cook overnight. There wasn't a tastier smell in the whole world. Then, carefully, he began to fill the stockings from his sack.

Upstairs, he thought he heard someone stirring. He could imagine what the tree looked like, how delighted Catherine and Frank would be when they came down to see their presents.

Outside, the snow still fell, softening the morning. He found the radio set and turned it on. Christmas carols sounded. The noises upstairs grew louder.

Travel certainly made you appreciate the simple things of life, he thought. His eyes filled with happy tears. He went to the kitchen cupboard and took out the bottle of Heine he had put there the night before. Frank hadn't found it. The seal was unbroken. Jerry helped himself to a little nip.

Mrs. Cornelius came thumping downstairs in her old carpet slippers. She wore a bright red and green dressing gown, her hair still in curlers, last night's make-up still smeared across her face. She rubbed her eyes, staring with approval at the lumpy stockings hanging over the stove. Behind her peered bleary Frank, Catherine's huge blue eyes, suspicious Colonel Pyat.

"Cor," she said. "Merry Christmas, love."

"Merry Christmas, mum." He leaned to kiss her. "God help us, one and all."

THE END

Parts of this story originally appeared in *Nature, Planet Stories, The New Statesman, Time, The Spectator, Gardens and Guns, Fantasy Spots, PC World, Wired, The Happy Mag, Boy's Friend Library, Schoolboy's Own Library, Popular Science, The Magnet, Nelson Lee Library, Sexton Blake Library, Union Jack Library, Good Housekeeping, Sports Illustrated, Texas Monthly, Harper's, The New Yorker, The New York Times, The Guardian, Novae Terrae*, and others.

MY LONDONS

THERE AREN'T MANY pictures of my childhood London. To get a glimpse of the world I grew up in, I have to give microscopic attention to the backgrounds of English movies made between 1945 and 1955 in the hope of seeing the ruined South Bank in *Hue and Cry* or the remains of Wapping in *Night and the City*. If I'm willing to sit through hours of Cockney stereotypes, I might occasionally catch a few meters of library footage shot through the windows of a tram with Sid James's head in the way.[1] My London is fleeting, mysterious, torn down or buried.

London was different up to 1940. From the illustrated books, it often seems tranquil and quaint, full of lost churchyards and hidden courts. There were always places where the traffic noise dropped away and you could enjoy a bit of peace. That was before the firestorms blasted the East End into blazing fragments of people and buildings, when so much of that quaint tranquillity became heaps of rubble, tottering walls, fire-blasted windows, cutaways of people's private lives: their bathrooms and bedrooms, everything they'd valued, exposed to the hasty curiosity of the survivors.

By 1945, the bodies and the worst of the rubble had been cleared away, and I see from those pathetic scraps of newsreels and pictures from the illustrated magazines the London I really loved and grew up in. Until then it had been a malleable London in which you could leave home in the morning and find your street completely transformed by the evening; where the house next door could become a pile of junk or your best friend could disappear forever. After the war finished, we knew what in some ways was a more innocent London. We hadn't quite taken in the Nazi Holocaust, let alone the A-bomb. We were a bit bewildered by how, having won, we were somehow poorer than when we were losing. The London in which Orwell wrote *1984* was my first peacetime London.

I wouldn't much want to live through that period again. Most of those films I give so much attention to were terrible, about keeping a stiff upper lip and knowing your place while facing down the Chaos. We kept replaying that trauma for years. What had gone wrong?

Our general entertainment was mostly dreadful and, like our styles, shrunken cheap imitations of what boom-time America was offering. The decade represents a world which has no representation in the physical world around me, for my ruins have vanished and the unfamiliar, often beautiful buildings erected in their place offer few coordinates from which to calibrate my memories.

By the time I had my first job as a messenger for a shipping company in the City, I could take a bus or a train down to the docks and then walk for miles looking for the appropriate ship or customs office, past grey cranes, redbrick warehouses, endless rust-grimed ships. I never had any idea of where docklands ended. Apart from the offices of great shipping lines, banks and insurance companies, the City was still an area of small businesses. There were scrapyards, independent stationers, booksellers, printers, chop houses, eel and pie shops, tea shops: a London whose variety and complexity you didn't have to guess at.

Then there were the places where London was simply

not—a few irregular mounds of grass and weeds with rusted wire sticking through concrete, like broken bones, exposed nerves. This part of London could very easily be identified because almost nothing of it had survived except the larger seventeenth- and eighteenth-century buildings like Tower Hill, the Customs House, the Mint, the Monument. And of course St. Paul's, her dome visible from the river as you came up out of the delicious stink of fresh fish from Billingsgate Market, a snap of cold in the bright morning, and walked between high banks of overgrown debris along lanes trodden to the contour of the land. We had made those paths by choosing the simplest routes through the ruins. Grass and moss and blazing purple fireweed grew in every chink. Sun glinted on Portland Stone, and to the west, foggy sunsets turned the river crimson. You never got lost. The surviving buildings themselves were the landmarks you used, like your eighteenth-century ancestors, to navigate from one place to the other.

Slowly, the big brutal blocks of concrete and fake Le Corbusier flats began to dwarf St. Paul's and the Royal Mint, and the familiar trails disappeared, together with the alleys and yards, the little coffee shops and printers. Like an animal driven from its natural environment, I'd turn a corner and run into a newly made cliff. The docks disappeared with astonishing speed. One day the ships were shadows honking out of the smog and the next they were gone. Airfreight and containers were replacing the old systems. Without our heavy exports we didn't need ships; without the ships we didn't need the docks.

West London, where I got my next job, is a lot easier to identify from 1950s Rex Harrison comedies. Almost everything was dark green and brass: motorcars, front doors, porters' uniforms. Everything else was bright yellow (driving caps, cars, frocks). Smart young voices imitated Noël Coward and Gertie Lawrence. and their owners buzzed about in MGs and Mayflowers. I worked for people rather like them. They completed my education. They gave me my taste for good food and wine and introduced me to T. S. Eliot and Proust. I was regarded as a bit of an *enfant terrible* and they encouraged me to write. I hardly had to work at all. For a while it was always maytime in Mayfair and spring in Park Lane. By the time I was seventeen, I was back in Holborn, editing *Tarzan Adventures*, where I'd sold most of my early work. But I'd added quite a lot to my social and literary education.

By then, too, I'd found Soho, jazz and skiffle, and had actually twice played washboard with the Vipers, who became the Shadows. I'd cut a demo (which set my musical career back for years) and I was hanging out with people who introduced me to Howlin' Wolf and Sonny Terry. I learned Woody Guthrie licks from Ramblin' Jack Elliot and corresponded with Guthrie and Seeger, under house arrest as un-Americans. I became more critical of politicians. My digs were in North Kensington and Fulham, which had sustained a bit more of the Blitz and were full of poor immigrants. There the streets were grey, dirty, hopeless, and often violent. I did wonder why all the posh bits of London were only what you might call lightly bombed, and why all the working-class suburbs were piles of ashy rubble. When Churchill (as he explained later) was sending back false intelligence about the Nazi strikes, suggesting that Streatham was the centre of our steelyards, he didn't seem too eager to give the impression that Belgravia was an industrial beehive. But I don't hate him for it. He did, after all, give me a lot to write about and a strong sense that nothing is permanent.

Soho was coffee bars and formica signs, formica tabletops. Formica hid all the old shop signs and looked at least superficially modern. Rock and roll, sex and drugs. Trad jazz became skiffle and skiffle became blues or R&B. I played guitar for a while in a whores' hotel. There were no proper threads in the shops. Just grey suits, tweed jackets, and corduroys. We took old stiff detachable collars and wore them with thin black ties, adding a car coat, white shirt, trousers stitched tight to our legs. My children say I was a Mod. I say those were the only clothes we had.

Around 1963 my wife and I moved to Colville Terrace,

where our next-door neighbour, a big knife-fighting whore called Marie, was regularly and noisily arrested nightly at about 2 AM. I took over *New Worlds* magazine, determined to lift from science fiction some fresh conventions, which J. G. Ballard, Barrington Bayley, and I felt were needed to reinvigorate English fiction.

My main contribution to this period of experiment was Jerry Cornelius, his name pinched from a greengrocer's sign in Notting Hill. As Mike Harrison pointed out, he was as much a technique, a narrative device, as a character.[2] Like me, Jerry relished ruins. Unlike me, he enjoyed making more of them. Through that era we called "the '60s"—which really ran from about 1963 with the Beatles first No. 1 single to around 1978 with Stiff's second tour—we continued to experiment in almost every field and genre. One of the reasons that period can't be reproduced is precisely because we hardly knew what we were doing. Now we probably know too much. We moved to a wonderful flat with a big leafy square behind it.

It was a wonderful time to have kids. I took them to music festivals and to little parks and museums, my secret boltholes like Derry and Tom's Famous Roof Garden where little old ladies met for tea after doing their shopping. None of these places had yet become self-conscious or been persuaded to exploit their "features." I knew we were enjoying a golden age that couldn't last, but I was determined we should get the most out of it. Even with strikes and hard economic times, we had the first Notting Hill Carnivals, numerous open-air gigs and a general improvement in local morale.

But we could already see the end coming. One afternoon I was in my back garden when a Liberal solicitor asked me if I was coming to a newly formed "gardens committee" meeting. When I told him I wasn't, he cheerfully informed me that that was my right. I told him that I knew what my rights were. I also sensed that this was definitely the beginning of the end.

By 1980, the Famous Roof Garden had become a private club. While it was still possible to lunch there, its casual nature had changed. Slowly I began to feel a stranger in my own city. I had, of course, been part of the gentrification process, but I didn't like the way people from the country and the suburbs were actually beginning to displace the locals. I like my classes mixed. We sold up and moved to Texas.

For all those years I lived around the Portobello Road, I learned that what people want more than authenticity is a provenance, a narrative. It wasn't enough to sell a modern flowery chamber pot as "Victorian," it had to be Oscar Wilde's chamber pot. The developers and remodelers soon learned this lesson. The formica signs were stripped away and old buildings were made to look older.

Good, innovative writers like Iain Sinclair and Peter Ackroyd with *White Chapell, Scarlet Tracings,* and *Hawksmoor,* aware of our need for authentic as well as virtual memory, linked the past with the present to show how the city shaped us. The media, particularly TV, picked up on the idea and soon had created "London," the character: golden-hearted London, whose dark spine was the Thames, whose dark soul was the Thames. This character appeared again and again, in all those sequels to famous Victorian novels or pastiches that spoke fruitily of Limehouse and Wapping.

Ackroyd played into this image, filmed for TV, lit from below, a bearded Dickens impersonator trotting in his wake, but Sinclair was having none of it. The first of London's psychogeographers, he headed for the M25, daring anyone who followed him to make something romantic from motorway cafes and discarded Big Mac boxes. While Ballard reflected on the curve of the Westway mirrored in suburban reservoirs, Sinclair peered into the bays underneath, searching for the remains of the population.

The rise of psychogeography was in some ways an impulse to rediscover those old natural paths I and others like me had trodden through the ruins, to find ways of rediscovering serious memory, something which Peter Ackroyd, Alan Moore, and Will Self understood.

As well as friends and relatives, who are also memory, we

are equally dependent on the geography of our cities for the myths and rituals by which we live. Without conscious ritual we have only buried tram tracks, some vague ideas of what still lies under the steel and concrete cladding, and a few bits of film.

I have nothing against virtuality. We create virtual identities for London. We create them for ourselves. We seek options allowing us to survive and, with luck, be happy. Jerry Cornelius knows, as he strolls in clothes just recently back in fashion, through virtual ruins, virtual futures, that it's the only way we'll survive, *as long as we're fully conscious*, so that when fashions like Dickens World cease to suit the tourists, we'll have another city standing by. I'm hoping for a London that neither swings nor sags, is neither grim nor gay, but rises defiantly, a fresh guarantee against the dying of our memories.

NOTES

1. South African comic actor known mainly for playing a London cockney.
2. But can't the same be said of Elizabeth Bennet?

"GET THE MUSIC RIGHT"

MICHAEL MOORCOCK INTERVIEWED BY TERRY BISSON

Why Texas?

I was on the run. Looking for some fresh mythology.

You have played a central role in science fiction since the editorship of New Worlds *magazine in the 1960s. How has that role changed from then to now?*

I suppose I was more of a gadfly in those days where SF was concerned. I'd read almost none of the so-called "Golden Age" (1950s) SF. I bought a long run of *Astounding* when I became editor of *New Worlds* because I thought I ought to look at it, and found most of it dull and unreadable. This was also the experience of J. G. Ballard and others who had expected far more of American SF than it actually delivered (apart from a relatively small amount found mostly in *Galaxy*).

American 1960s "New Wave" was about improving the quality of SF, but we Brits were less interested in that than we were in using SF methodology to look at the contemporary world. SF magazines were the only ones that liked our ideas, but we had to provide rationalizations to those stories, more or less. Explication dulled down the vision.

Fritz Leiber, whom I greatly admired, told me that he and several of his contemporaries like Bloch and Kuttner had the same problem in their day. So you'd write, say, an absurdist story but you could only sell it if you added: "On Mars . . ." or "In the future . . ." and then stuck in a boring rationalization.

Anyway, we could only really publish in the SF magazines.

But we also felt contemporary fiction was anaemic and had lost the momentum modernism had given it. Most fiction we saw had no way it could usefully confront modern concerns—the H-bomb, computers, engineering and communications advances, space travel—not to mention changing social conventions and consequently language, politics, warfare, the altered psyche in the face of so much novelty of experience.

Almost all the literary fiction we read was actually retrospective (Durrell, Heller, Roth, or Bellow) or only pretending to tackle contemporary issues in a novel way (Selby, B. S. Johnson, the Beats, and others who saw themselves as the most interesting subject matter).

The reason we liked William Burroughs (*Naked Lunch*) was because his language focused on modern times and drew much of its vitality from modern idiom. We were inspired by him and Borges rather than influenced by them.

Many of our heroes (French existentialists, *nouvelle vague* movies) read SF and the *Galaxy* writers in particular (Bester, Dick, Sheckley, Pohl and Kornbluth, and, of course, Bradbury). In the 1950s there was far more acceptance of American SF in European intellectual circles than in the United States itself, where that retrospective tone spells "literature" to the *New Yorker* reader and in my view is the bane of American fiction, especially when linked to regionalism/provincialism.

Emerging from World War II into Austerity Britain, it was easy for us to see *1984* all around us. The three *New Worlds* writers generally linked in those days (and I was even then more writer than editor) were myself, Ballard, and Brian Aldiss. I'd come out of the London Blitz, Ballard from the Japanese civilian prison camps, and Aldiss from the war in Malaya, and we all had reason to welcome the A-bomb, perceiving it with far more ambiguity than most.

Post-1946 modernity was a bit on the grim side, but we felt that as writers we'd been given an amazing box of tools, an array of subjects never before available to literature, and we used those tools and subjects in ways that tended to celebrate postwar experience rather than denigrate it.

Our tastes in SF were often different. Brian liked *Astounding,* while I just couldn't read it. Ballard liked Bradbury. I preferred good pulp like Brackett and Bester. Richard Hamilton, the pop artist, thought all three of us were damaging the kind of stuff he liked. He'd used Robby the Robot at his first important exhibition at the Whitechapel Gallery.

I couldn't continue today to have the role I had then, because what we hoped would happen *has* happened. SF methods and subjects are now incorporated into modern fiction in order to deal with modern matters. Nostalgia is largely the preserve of fantasy and so-called Steampunk. (I suggested in a recent review that it really should be called Steam Opera since it has so many lords and ladies in it.)

Anyway: Then my role was to attack the old and celebrate the new. Now my role is to be careful not to discourage new writers. In my old age I carry a burden, if you like, of gravitas! This makes me a kinder critic.

An Elric film has been in the works (or not) for years. What's the current status? Any other Hollywood interest?

The Weitz brothers and Universal had Elric under option for some time, but I have no idea what's happening now. Michael Bassett, the English director who made *Solomon Kane,* is now interested. I've corresponded with him a bit, but to be honest, I don't much care about movies and tend to show little interest when I'm approached. I suspect Bassett would be a good choice, though.

You started out writing for comics, then dropped it until the mid-1990s (and Multiverse*). Do you still like the form? Why?*

I wrote a lot of commercial comics for Fleetway as a kid, but by the 1960s I'd had enough of what I regarded as a primitive medium. I had problems with the low-level racism/stereotyping prevalent at the time and found myself at odds with my bosses—refusing to write World War II comics, for instance. I wrote a bit of picture-journalism attacking what I saw as the trend of grown-ups to elevate juvenile forms, (especially in France) such as *Barbarella*.

Of course, I'd dusted off my old comic skills to write the Jerry Cornelius material for *International Times* in the late '60s/early '70s, and I'd done a Hawkwind strip with Jim Cawthorn for *FRENDZ,* another underground newspaper. I did quite a lot with the underground in the '60s and '70s.

Then along came Alan Moore, and I saw that it was possible to use comics in a fun, adult way in a commercial environment—as long as you had a good collaborator, as I did. By then I was friends with Alan, and you could say it was his example, as well as meeting a bunch of very bright kids at the San Diego Comic Convention, that made me want to get back into the medium.

So when I was asked to do a comic for DC I decided to try something ambitious, running three main stories at the same time and having them link up at the end.

That was *Michael Moorcock's Multiverse* in which I developed my ideas about a possible multiverse in which context determined identity, utilizing some Chaos Theory and Mandelbrotian notions of self-similarity.

I really like to carry fairly complex ideas in comics or, say, in the Doctor Who novel I'm just now finishing. Maybe to stop myself taking such notions too seriously. The clockwork multiverse.

Have you adapted other people's work for comics?

Well, only if you count Hal Foster. I "translated" the Spanish version of his Tarzan script back into English, mostly by guesswork, during my first publishing job on *Tarzan Adventures*. Oh, and I also did a two-part Tom Strong (Alan Moore's character).

You used to listen to the Grateful Dead while writing? Who do you listen to now, if anyone?

Grateful Dead. Messiaen. Mozart. Dylan. Mahler. John Prine. New Riders. John Fogarty. Ravel. Schoenberg. Ives. Chet Baker. Williams. Elgar. Grateful Dead. Robert Johnson. Howlin' Wolf. Glenn Miller. Noël Coward. Beatles. Gus Elen. Grateful Dead. Next question.

That last one's not a group, it's an exit strategy.

In one of your novels (I forget which one), Charon, ferryman of the River Styx, explains and justifies himself by saying, "It's a steady job." Have you ever regretted not having a steady nine-to-fiver?

I started out doing nine-to-five jobs—messenger for a shipping company at fifteen, "junior consultant" (office boy) for a firm of management consultants, and editorial jobs (*Tarzan Adventures, Sexton Blake Library, Current Topics*). I've never regretted it. I'd hate to do it again.

Ever heard of writer's block? How do you deal with it? Or do you ever have to?

I've heard of it. Never really had it. My answer is to go into a different character, scene, etc. If you determine your scheme first, you usually know what's supposed to go where and when. Structure informs plot elements. Get the "music" right, too: what you hear in your mind. I tried to talk about some of this in *Death Is No Obstacle*, the interview I did with Colin Greenland in the 1990s.

Where the hell is the Multiverse? Are there entrances? What about exits?

It's everywhere. We're in it. No way in. No way out. No centre and near-infinite centres. Just points of entrance through the Second Ether. I first mentioned it in "The Sundered Worlds" in *SF Adventures*, 1962. Black Holes, but I didn't call them that. I don't like too much explication generally, but I've done quite a bit in my Doctor Who novel due out in October 2010.

Have you had run-ins with censorship? Or is SF too far under the literary radar? (I liked your comment about Bradbury's Fahrenheit 451: "Why bother to burn books when you can make them disappear?")

I've been censored in America more than anywhere else. First by Avon in *The Final Programme* (1967). The worst was by Random House in *Byzantium Endures* when they slashed a lot of the antisemitism from a book that is primarily about the Nazi Holocaust. NAL got nervous and made me change Reagan to Eagan in their version of *The Warlord of the Air*. Their lawyers got on it and did what lawyers do. Of course *Byzantium* isn't SF and I didn't regard the Cornelius stuff as SF, either.

Oh, and there's a version of *The Adventures of Una Persson and Catherine Cornelius* which was very thoroughly censored, along with another book whose title I forget, by the publisher. America has a free speech clause in her Constitution, unlike Britain, but Americans tend to self-censor in ways not generally found in France and England.

What do you do for fun? (besides write . . .)

Due to my wounded foot, in recent years I've talked, eaten, and gone to movies (I live part of the time in Paris, where movies are worth going to).

Now that my foot's better, I'll add "walking" (though these days I'm more a *flaneur* than a fifteen-mile-hiker). I used to enjoy mountain climbing a lot and "fell-driving," in which you take a big, preferably high-powered sedan up onto what are commonly considered hiking trails.

I am especially proud of being one of the only three people to drive England's Pennine Way in an on-road (2WD) vehicle. The other two were in the same car with me—Jon Trux and Bob Calvert. Hikers used to get outraged and curse us as we roared past.

RE: Your time with the band Hawkwind: You once spoke of what a pleasure it was to walk out on stage and see a whole crowd of people eagerly awaiting your appearance. Do you ever have that experience as a writer? Or is it the opposite?

I do love the stage. I'd have been a performer if I hadn't been a writer. I love reading and signing sessions too. I like people. A solo reading is harder work than playing in a band because in a band you have your mates to cover your fluffs.

But when I'm writing, I want the nearest thing to a monk's cell as possible. A friend once phoned when I was in the middle of a paragraph and I picked up the phone because I thought it might be Linda. "Bugger off!" I told him. "That's no way to speak to a friend," he said. "You can't be a friend," I said. "A friend wouldn't be phoning me while I'm working."

I hate people when I'm writing.

There is a subtheme of incest that runs through the JC (Jerry Cornelius) books. He is in love with his sister (before he kills her), and the deliciously strange Jherek Carnelian is in a romantic relationship with his mom. What gives?

Nothing much. I never had any siblings. Wish fulfilment? I probably just like the romantic/decadent flavour. Jerry also resurrects his sister, don't forget.

The critic Lorna Sage once said that I had too many "sleeping sisters" in my work (I think she was reviewing *Mother*

London, which has a major female character asleep and dreaming through much of the book) and suggested that I preferred passive women.

A canard. All my women friends are far from passive. Hilary, my first wife, was by no means passive; neither is Linda, far from it; and my female friends like Angela Carter, Andrea Dworkin, and others, are/were all pretty aggressive/active.

The sleeping sister could be a holdover from the screamer-who-needs-rescuing convention of popular fiction.

Besides Elric and Corum, the Eternal Champions, and Cornelius, who seems to be a more high-tech version of the same, there is also Pyat, the cranky Russky of Byzantium. *How does he fit into your pantheon—or does he?*

Cornelius does what fantasy heroes can't do easily. I wanted him to confront contemporary stuff. He's far more knowing than standard fantasy heroes. I never regarded him as an SF character, let alone fantasy. The books were never published as fantasy or genre at all in England, but rather as straight "experimental" novels (I preferred to call them unconventional). I used Jerry to look at modern life.

Pyat was designed, or created if you will, for a very different purpose, though he originally appeared as a relatively minor character in the Cornelius quartet. I had felt compelled for some time to confront the Nazi Holocaust full-on (I have my share of survival guilt) and Pyat turned out to be the right guy for the job.

Pyat believes in systems. He sees society as a "correctable" machine. He is a modern man, if you like, in search of a soul. He represents the twentieth century's belief that society is a machine, which only needs the right engineering approach to make life perfect. In that sense his story riffs off "hard" SF of the kind you used to find in lots of pre-1940s visionary fiction. Wells grew increasingly to write this kind of utopian fantasy, and of course it is in Gernsback and all kinds of American stuff. Not only was society a machine that would respond to the right engineering—humankind itself was perfectible through the kind of genetic theories to be found in American and European thinking between the two world wars. Hitler based a lot of his "reasoning" on theories prevalent in the United States in particular, just as he based many of his racial laws on ideas first put into practice in America. Stalin had similar ideas and was also inspired by Hitler's methods. Mussolini, too, thought society and human individuals could be improved just as we improved planes, cars, and trains to go faster, be safer, not to mention more comfortable.

Hell, even Woody Guthrie sang about the power of electricity to improve our lives. The Grand Coulee Dam. Anarchists, too, subscribed to a slightly different and perhaps more humane vision of human society with the "right" systems in place.

It's against all this that Pyat is playing—as well as his terror, originally infecting him as a Jew in the Ukraine. (I've written more about the conception of Pyat in *The Daily Telegraph*, which can be found online at my website, Moorcock's Miscellany, in the Q&A section under published writing, or at the *Telegraph* site under Books: "A Million Betrayals.") Pyat was written from a sense of payback, of duty, a compulsion to use my talent to examine what was the single greatest crime of the twentieth century and see how it was allowed to come about.

Pyat claims to be many things that he isn't—an Aryan, an engineering genius, and so on. He's an unreliable narrator in a carefully reconstructed version of our own world. Cornelius is not unreliable in that sense (and neither are Elric and Co.) and readers are only invited to examine his actions from their own perspective of events.

It's an ongoing theme, if you like: I'm always asking if Romance is some specific kind of lie.

Your career spans the gap between the typewriter and the word processor. At what point did you make the switch? What was that like?

I was using a Selectric II for years. I still have it. I still have an Imperial 50/60 produced during World War II and a Smith

Corona portable (should electricity fail). All my work from the age of nine was done on the Imperial.

Soon after I got to Texas in 1994, I was asked by ORIGIN, a game company, to write an original game that could also be a movie and a book. I wasn't sure of the scheme, but I liked the challenge.

At one point they asked me what kind of computer I was using. I told them I didn't have one. At this, an embarrassed silence fell across the room. At last the guy running the firm cleared his throat and asked, "Would you mind if we got you one?"

"You can get me one," I said, "but I can't say I'd use it."

So it duly arrived and within twenty-four hours, I'd taken to it like a duck to water. They were delighted. I wrote my first story on the computer within two days of getting it (a Cornelius short). They'd gotten me the top of the line, of course, and asked me what I thought of it. I said it was like a non-driver being given a Rolls-Royce and then being asked what he thought of it.

Mandelbrot supplied me with a map of my brain. Word supplied me with new applications.

What's your relationship to the very lively Austin music scene? Who do you hang out with in Texas? Writers? Rednecks? Ex-prezzes? Out-of-work musicians?

A few of my friends are musicians. Most of the people I know here I met through local politics and suchlike. Leftist activists in Texas really know the score. One of my best friends, Jewell Hodges, is ninety-two and has been involved in civil rights most of her life. She started life working in fields at the age of twelve, shoving cotton into sacks longer than she was tall.

Almost as soon as we got here, Linda was co-opted onto the local Family Crisis Centre board, and with another woman set about transforming it, with accommodation for threatened spouses and children, outreach, education, and so on; and I supported her in that, being an active pro-feminist.

We also got involved with the local food pantry, which Jewell was running when we got here. She asked me how we fed our hungry poor in the UK. I thought for a bit until I realized that we didn't actually have poverty in the UK of the kind she was battling in Texas.

Texas has no income tax and you feel obliged to involve yourself in activities which, as a European, you believe should be supported by taxes. So I self-tithe to balance that out. I know a few others who do.

Most of my musician friends in Austin start their gigs too late for an old man like me who has a long drive home afterwards! I did perform once or twice with pals in Austin.

I know a few writers—Howard Waldrop, for instance—whom I get on with. Though I have a few friends who are writers, I don't hang out with them much. It was the same in the UK and in France. I tend to be very loyal to my friends and maybe for that reason I don't have many close friends. But they're mostly from different walks of life. I enjoy company but am essentially a loner.

Do you ever go back and loot your works for ideas? Do you read your early stuff at all?

Very rarely. I almost never reread a book. I riff off the fundamental ideas underlying my books—multiverse, eternal champions, context defining characters, and so on. In the old days I'd write one draft in three days and have a friend read it for typos, possible inconsistencies, and I've never reread those. I've made a few revisions when readers point out plot errors or loopy inconsistencies, of course. A few of those early fantasies got to the bookstores without *anyone* having read them—me, editors, publicists.

I tend to have a good memory for books I've done, as if they were memories of my real life, though; so when it comes to sequels I seem to be able to take up a sequel pretty much where I left off. I have a terrible memory yet seem to remember books pretty easily.

Reading my own work is a fast cure for insomnia. Linda will confirm this. When I can't sleep, I go to get something by me and am dozing within a minute or two. This makes proof-reading very hard.

If you were casting a Cornelius movie, who would play Jerry? Did you know he's from my hometown?

You're from Notting Hill? Not sure who—but Tilda Swinton is still my favourite choice. Someone did a Photoshop of her as Elric, which also worked very well. That's in the Image Gallery on my site, I think.

I was thinking about Johnny Depp.

Him too. But he's too busy playing pirate these days.

What kind of car do you drive? (I ask this of everyone.) Did you have a car in the Old Country?

We have an old Lexus SUV, which we bought new and cheap when my leg needed more room because of the wound, and that was about the only car that would take me.

I briefly owned a beautiful Citroën classic convertible with running boards and stuff. In the 1970s, I had a massive Nash (that's what I conquered the Pennine Way in), which in England was like driving a bus. I bought it because it could take a load of children and a load of band members.

But after our Fiat, we mostly had a Honda Civic in the UK. Linda made me stop driving when she discovered I didn't have a license. I'm useless at tests and exams. So although the driving instructor said all I needed were a couple of lessons and I'd sail through, I got worse and worse as we went along and gave it up as a lost cause.

Texas is littered with Lost Causes.

We mostly used public transport in London and we still use mostly public transport in France and the rest of Europe. I'm still an advocate for good public systems. One of my reasons for moving to Texas was because the then Democratic state governor wanted to bring a TGV to Texas and a light rail system for Austin.

I was *very* disappointed when Bush became governor.

You floated an interesting concept in Gloriana *when you said that modern art's relentless demand for novelty made bad artists worse, but good artists better. How does that work?*

I don't remember writing that! I can see how it might work, though. I think there are plenty of good journeyman painters and scriveners whose talents are wasted by attempted novelty. I was probably thinking of what happened on *New Worlds* when perfectly good run-of-the-mill writers tried to produce what they thought were New Wave stories and came up with crap, whereas good writers who were encouraged to expand (Disch, Aldiss, Ballard) produced superb stuff.

Do you regard the fact that SF is still a commercially viable literature a help or a hindrance?

It doesn't matter a lot. I liked it better before publishers didn't know what sold. There was a good patch that lasted into the 1980s even, when publishers were so uncertain about what the public liked that they were willing to give almost anything a go. By the 1990s, they'd worked out what sold and what didn't, and you saw a slowing down of interesting offbeat material and a tendency for categories and sub-categories of generic stuff to become the norm.

I think it gets harder and harder to sell new stuff—stuff that breaks conventions —because now publishers and booksellers "know the market" and know what will sell (i.e., what *did* sell). So the chances of selling an offbeat novel masquerading in a commercial form get slimmer all the time.

I liked SF precisely for that potential for masquerade—avant-garde pretending to be space opera . . .

Ever get through The Faerie Queene? Ulysses?

Yes. *Gloriana* riffed off *The Faerie Queene. Ulysses* is best enjoyed when read aloud, as is Proust. But if you can read *Pamela* by Richardson or *One of Our Conquerors* by Meredith, you can probably read anything. It's books like *Dune* or *Lord of the Rings* that I find almost unreadable.

You are one of SF's most "literary" writers, and at the same time a militant populist in literature, opposed to high-canon thinking. How do you reconcile those roles?

By demonstration.

An innovative artist must create his own audience as he goes. Do you see yourself as an educator or an entertainer? ("Both" is a cheat.)

Both. I have been both most of my life. I've had magazines in which I could present arguments, publish examples. I used to say that the whole *New Worlds* thing was designed to create an audience for the kind of stuff that Ballard, myself, and others wanted to write.

I think we did that.

My entertainments always contain some sort of confrontational elements; my more confrontational stories have large elements of comedy in particular, and I'd say that was reasonably entertaining.

What do you think of McEwan? Austen? Wells?

McEwan, who is vaguely interesting for his subject matter, tends to dodge the issues like much middlebrow fiction and can be a bloody awful writer. As I can be.

Austen's a joy.

Wells is brilliant, often irritating. I have pretty much an entire collection of Wells, most of them firsts and in the original magazines from *The Time Machine* on. I have all of Austen in a nice edition. I have no McEwan, Amis (*fils* or *père*), and no Rushdie. I have all of Elizabeth Bowen, Angus Wilson, Colette, and plenty of Elizabeth Taylor, Rose MacAulay, and lots of Edwardian realists; all of Meredith, Eliot, Dickens; all of Stevenson, Conrad, lots of Ford Maddox Ford, Jack London, Howells, Harte, Twain, California writers who could listen to the eloquence of the streets; a fair amount of Saul Bellow, and a bunch of contemporary writers. Today's English pantheon is pretty miserable in comparison.

You once said that your first approach to SF was a determination not to be marginalized. Was that the idea behind New Worlds*? Did it work?*

To a degree. I'm far less marginalized in the UK, I think, where a lot more of my non-generic fiction has been published, won prizes and so forth. I get lengthy reviews for books that aren't presented as generic. I'm certainly not marginalized in that sense.

My first hardcovers in England generally got good reviews. *Behold the Man* and *The Final Programme* weren't reviewed as genre fiction. Only with the flood of fantasy paperbacks did people begin to get confused, I think. But *Gloriana* was extensively reviewed as non-generic.

I tend to get treated according to the level of ambition people see in my books. I can be included, for instance, in a *Times* list of the fifty best writers since the end of World War II but still condescended to as some kind of literary barbarian by academics unfamiliar with my stuff. I'm comfortable with that.

I think I make some critics and academics a bit uneasy. If you look at a copy of *New Worlds* from 1967 on you'll see that a general audience is consistently addressed. I wouldn't let contributors address the "SF field." Reviewers reviewed Ballard and Borges together, but had to address the general reader. We never spoke of that "field" in which I always imagined a bunch of sheep chewing and rechewing the same grass.

Many readers didn't know *New Worlds* had ever been a genre magazine. We were accepted almost from the start as a literary magazine. Ballard, Aldiss, Disch, and myself were frequently on radio and TV speaking for what the critics termed "the new SF." An anthology was prepared with this name. It attracted a wide readership amongst what you could call the English intelligentsia, particularly those who had liked, say, *Galaxy*, but needed something a bit posher in appearance to legitimize their enthusiasm.

We were fashionable in the 1960s the way the pop artists (some of whom were featured in *New Worlds*) and modern poets were fashionable. It was strange to come to the United States and find science fiction still marginalized, still condescended to. Snobbery seems much stronger in the United States, especially in New York.

But it's the same with rock and roll, I think. In the UK rock and SF were often linked —lots of musicians read SF, some writers performed in bands. I think we can see a major improvement even in America now, though. Writers like Michael Chabon have done much to force snobs to revalue—though I notice he's been attacked here for his enthusiasm for generic fiction.

I sometimes think America is now the *old* World as far as the arts and politics and social ideas are concerned.

Did you line edit at New Worlds*?*

Not really. There's a different approach in the UK and the United States, I think. American editing tends to come out of the newspaper tradition and seems excessive to me. If we had a problem I'd usually xerox the page or pages in question and underline queries to see what the author felt.

A curmudgeon (MM) once said that today's SF had gotten too sophisticated to take chances. Do you still make that charge?

Well, I always drew my inspiration from pulp and never much liked the movement to make SF "respectable" (which might seem odd, reading the above). I hated that as much as I hated the movement to make black people whiter. My attitude was "like this or prove yourself a backward idiot."

So if we're talking about sophistication as respectability, I have to say it makes me miserable. The more invisible you are, the more chances you feel able to take. Rock 'n' roll, SF, and comics always show this, I think. Most artistic innovation comes through popular media or at least through obscure media. I chose SF and R&R precisely because there was no one looking over your shoulder when you did it—no critical magazines to study it.

Not when I started, anyway. There was just *Crawdaddy*.

You once suggested that anyone who wants to write fantasy should quit reading your stuff and read Mervyn Peake instead. Does that career plan still hold?

I didn't say Peake in particular, but yes, it still holds. If you want to write SF/fantasy, read everything but those genres. Peake is in many ways more in the absurdist tradition I've always liked—Peacock, Jarry, Firbank, Vian, Peake. Even William Burroughs is an absurdist first, I think.

You're a musician as well as a writer. Do you still play? What? What was the state of popular music in England in the 1960s? Did "modern" (Miles, Monk, Mingus) jazz play a role in your postmodern liberation, or was it all rock?

It was all rock and modern composers like Messiaen. In the '60s it was still possible not to have to book tickets for Schoenberg, he was so unpopular. This changed during that decade.

I didn't much care for jazz after a brief craze for it in the '50s, when in Paris you could hear a dozen greats in bars up and down one tiny street. Now I appreciate it much more and like it better. My tastes have broadened. I used to think only string quartets were worth listening to.

SF has been swamped by Fantasy. Are you partly to blame for that or do your consider your work a counterforce?

I write fantasy with more of an SF sensibility, I think. I write anti-fantasy. When Tolkien and I were really the only games in town, we both got our own nametag in bookstores, separate from the SF shelves. When Tolkienesque fantasy began to dominate I was knocked off the shelves by a bunch of Terries (nothing personal to you or Pratchett). That is, I sold when there wasn't a more escapist, comfortable brand.

Now I still sell pretty well, but it seems to be more to fantasy readers who don't much like Tolkien (or at least his clones).

The change in the United States came really when Donald Wollheim pirated the *Lord of the Rings* books and also found that *A Princess of Mars* wasn't in copyright. Larry Shaw at Lancer liked Jack Vance and me and was the first to publish my fantasy in the United States. I think my stuff probably is a counterforce at some level.

I don't think I'm to blame for Prof. T. My influences among modern writers were almost wholly American—Poul Anderson, Sprague de Camp, Fritz Leiber, C. L. Moore, Leigh Brackett, Robert E. Howard, Jack Vance.

Tolkien question here. The answer is "certainly." You provide the question.

Is Tolkien a sentimentalist who, like many writers (Sherriff, Deeping, etc.) emerging from World War I needed to mystify and sentimentalize that conflict and/or their part in it. To make "sacrifice" noble. Are you sympathetic to but irritated by such attitudes which spilled over into the English middle-class sensibility so that they lasted (via BBC drama, for instance) long after the end of World War II?

Rowling question here. The answer is "perhaps." You provide the question.

Has Rowling discovered a strategy for continuing that especially English genre, the public school story (Thomas Hughes, Talbot Baines Reade, Charles Hamilton, and many others), thus successfully continuing to spread certain English class attitudes well into the 21st century and across the world?

Do you wear a hat when you write? Do you have a regular work regimen? Coffee or tea?

I wear different hats. Currently I'm wearing a FLASH baseball cap for my Doctor Who novel. I prefer to work outside whenever possible and then I wear a wide-brimmed Panama.

Do you stay in touch with the old New Worlds *crowd (Sallis, Aldiss, Platt, Spinrad, Malzberg, etc.)? Why are they so grumpy?*

Are they? I'm scarcely in touch with anyone but Aldiss and Spinrad, and they seem actually less grumpy on most issues than they were in the '60s. They were always fairly confrontational by nature, as I am.

I grumpily want to know why Malzberg pinched the title of my novel *Breakfast in the Ruins*. I'm not in touch with him at all or I'd ask him myself. Maybe they're grumpy because all their bloody mates are dying. That pisses me off too.

Why was the New Wave such a Guy Thing? Or was it?

Not for want of trying to publish women. We published as many women as we could encourage—Emshwiller, Arnason, Sargent, Zoline, Castell (Vivienne Young in art), and of course Hilary Bailey. Would you count Doris Lessing?

You have to publish by example, if possible, and I know we tried to publish women, but they were thin on the ground.

Judith Merril was strongly associated with the so-called New Wave. Much of the fiction I write and we published was decidedly pro-women in a way that a lot of guy fiction (the Beats, for instance) was not.

Precisely the reason I can't enjoy either Amis. There's always been a distinct smell of the saloon bar in much fiction. Could be why my "default" writer, the one I always turn to when I can't think of anyone else to read, is Elizabeth Bowen (especially *Death of the Heart*).

My close friend Andrea Dworkin loved SF and wrote some, and we sometimes discussed this. She thought there were a lot more women published now because women don't tend to submit work where they think it isn't wanted. Given that Joanna Russ, Ursula Le Guin, and others are associated with the so-called New Wave, I'm not sure that it was such a guy thing!

I always wanted something ambitious from Joanna.

Disch became somewhat bitter toward SF. In your Humble Opinion, was this critical or personal?

Tom was always a bit confused on this issue. He wanted literary respectability more than any other author I knew and used to say "*The New Yorker* can smell the SF on me." (I just wrote a story touching on this, called "Stories" for an anthology called *Stories*.)

Once, when I got a full-page review in the *Times Literary Supplement* praising a book, Tom called me and said, "Congratulations. You've *won*!" I was baffled.

Tom was competitive, but he wanted his success to come from conventional institutions. He was far more a modern than a postmodern. He liked to think of himself as Henry James rather than Henry Kuttner. Yet he could be very generous and encouraging to new writers of SF.

He was always a snob, but never enough to hang out happily with other snobs. He was unhappy in New York, which is probably the snottiest town in the world, yet he hung on there wishing to be accepted—or accepted more.

That wasn't why he killed himself, though, I think. Essentially he killed himself because his partner Charles Naylor had died, leaving him terribly alone.

I was very fond of Charlie, but he was a worse snob than Tom in some ways, though much more "liberal" in some ways (anti-Jewish attitudes aside).

Unlike, say, Ballard who became increasingly radical into old age, Tom became increasingly reactionary until even the *Weekly Standard* (for which he wrote regularly) found some of his stuff went too far.

Is England or the United States more receptive to (or at least forgiving of) satire?

The tradition seems to have remained healthier in the UK than in the U.S., though that said, there are some fine American satirists.

I don't know. Americans seem to place a higher value on *politesse* than the British. We're far more savage toward public figures. This is odd since Free Speech isn't in our Bill of Rights.

I always have found it strange that Americans have to signal irony or humour in general by adding "joke" at the end of whatever they've said. Or by signalling quote marks. I've found I have to do it too sometimes or people take what I've said seriously. This spelling out of an ironic or sarcastic remark doesn't happen in England or France.

What do you read for fun?

Sexton Blake "story papers" (equivalent of dime novels) and others from between the wars. P. G. Wodehouse and a whole bunch of Edwardian comic/realist writers like Zangwill, Pett Ridge, Barry Paine, F. Anstey, Jerome K. Jerome. Scott, Q, Stevenson.

Do you read or write poetry?

Yes. Most of the poetry in my fiction, though, is parody (as in "Ernest Wheldrake," Swinburne's pseudonym under which he attacked his own work, as "Colvin" attacked mine). Otherwise I'm a crap poet.

You have written series novels, standalones, and short stories. What do you think is the distinction between short story writers and novelists?

Do you want me to be facetious? I suspect short story writers are temperamentally less patient than novelists.

Do you ever outline? Do you work from plot or character?

Not an outline as such, though I had to do one for the BBC when writing the Doctor Who novel they commissioned. I make extensive notes and then hardly ever refer to them. I tend to work from character, even with my fantasy novels. Writing Doctor Who was awkward in this respect since there's only so much you can do to work up his character.

Have you ever written a conventional screenplay? Do you like the form? (I do.)

I wrote one for *The Land That Time Forgot* and rewrote *The Final Programme*, and I've written a few that were never made. Usually I don't enjoy working with directors, though.

I'm used to doing a story and then standing or falling by it, whereas I get frustrated when I finish a job and someone comes along to tell me it's not quite right ("It's wonderful, Michael. There are just a *few* changes we thought of . . .") My theory is that having to work this way didn't help Fitzgerald or Faulkner stay (or even get) on the wagon. I'd be a drunk in similar circumstances.

The money's good but there's a reason for that.

Your narratives are known for their velocity. Does this mean they are speedy to write as well?

I used to feel, as a journalist, that over three days on a book was uneconomical, so all my fantasies took three days to write. I'd support myself with journalism. *Behold the Man* took five days. *The Final Programme* took ten. The longest it took me to write a book before *Byzantium Endures* was six weeks (*Gloriana*). *Byzantium* took six months.

These days it can take maybe a month for a first draft of a fantasy, with about two weeks for revision. Until *Byzantium* I rarely did more than one draft.

You describe yourself as an anarchist rather than a Marxist. What does this mean politically? Personally? Artistically?

It's a philosophical/moral position from which I can easily make quick decisions of pretty much every kind. My anarchism informs my pro-feminism, for instance.

I happen to believe as a writer that words are action and that we have to be able to stand by our actions and accept any consequences of our actions.

Therefore if someone tells me they have been, for example, raped by someone claiming to have been encouraged by my work, I feel I have to examine that work to see if it can't be changed.

If someone tells me they hate or are dissatisfied by a book of mine, I tend to send them their money back.

I modified the Cornelius books as I went along because too many young men were poncing about thinking it was cool to pose around being "amoral." Like many writers attracted to SF, I'm intensely moralistic.

What has living in the United States brought to your work as an artist?

A little more understanding of a country which is often baffling to Europeans because they feel it should be a better version of Europe—certainly better than the Europe settlers left behind. That it is in several ways a worse version is a bit of a shock to us.

The anti-intellectual tradition and the over-intellectualized tradition are both a bit depressing.

The tendency to live in enclaves concerns me. But the language of the South and Southwest gave me some good music for books like *Blood.*

Do you see anything stirring in contemporary SF outside the English language (United States and England)?

Not really. French SF and Indian SF are at last beginning to establish their own idioms, which is encouraging.

Some would say SF, like rock 'n' roll, has aged and is no longer the province of youth. Do you agree? Can this be reversed? Should it be?

It depends on what youth finds in it. I don't think you can bring the '60s/'70s back. I know, however, that if I was sixteen in this world I wouldn't be looking to SF or contemporary pop music for inspiration.

My first novel, Wyrldmaker, *was a Moorcock (Corum) imitation. Do I owe you an apology, or him? Or do you owe me one?*

You owe me one (for that 'y' in world). I loved your second novel, the one about the South. One of my absolute favourites.

Wow. Let's leave that in. How many projects do you generally have going at once? Is this a plan or lack of same?

Usually one novel or sequence of novels at a time, sometimes two or three (three at the moment). A short story or two. I'm usually writing a feature of some kind—a review, article or "diary" (I do a few a year for English newspapers, primarily the

Guardian or the *Financial Times*. Maybe a comic, a memoir, an introduction and so on. Usually at least one music project.

Does SF have a future? Or is it just reworking of old tropes? What writers do you see today as more forward-looking, i.e., is there any new ground to break? This is a trick question.

That depends entirely on the individual whose imagination is sparked by a form. I know one intensely modernist intellectual writer, who used to be part of a well-known Oxford literary crew, who taught himself physics because he felt he should know about such stuff. Who then wrote an excellent and convincing time travel story, which appeared in *Asimov's*.

SF definitely has a canon, and your works are embedded in it. Is there anyone left out or overlooked that you would add?

I'm not sure. I have read very little SF since, say, 1964. If Harness isn't in the canon I think he should be.

Delete?

Oh, well. There's always some you feel are overrated. I've never understood the appeal of most "Golden Age" writers. In the end a good stylist will remain included, I'd guess—like Bradbury—while the clunkier writers will slowly disappear. Style tends to last, even when at first rejected (Hammett, Faulkner, Peake, Ballard) by the lit establishment.

Have you ever "taught" (academically) SF as literature?

I have never taught anything directly (oh—I taught my daughters to punch and to shoot!) but editing is a bit like teaching in that you try to find out precisely what the author's wanting to say and help them say it. But I don't believe I *can* teach, except by example.

I was asked to write a book on technique a few years ago and said I don't know any rules for writing. All I could do was tell someone how I'd solved a problem in the hope it would be of some use to them.

If you taught a survey course on SF that covered four novels and five short stories, what would they be?

Bring the Jubilee, maybe, *The Drowned World, A Canticle for Leibowitz, The Time Machine*. Short stories by Fritz Leiber, Bradbury, Wells, M. J. Harrison's, Forster . . .

Any regrets so far?

What about? This interview?

I sometimes wish I hadn't written quite so many fantasy novels and spent a bit more time on stuff I took more seriously, like *Mother London*.

I let obsession with work affect relationships too much, I think.

The fantasy sequence I'm writing now is about the romantic lure of the exotic and how it can sometimes take your attention away from more important stuff, like politics and people.

BIBLIOGRAPHY

NOVELS

The Hungry Dreamers; lost manuscript—never published
Stormbringer (1965); restored and revised (1978)
The Sundered Worlds (1965) a.k.a. *The Blood Red Game* (1970)
The Fireclown (1965) a.k.a. *The Winds of Limbo* (1969)
Warriors of Mars (1965) a.k.a. *City of the Beast* (1970); as Edward P. Bradbury
Blades of Mars (1965) a.k.a. *Lord of the Spiders* (1971); as Edward P. Bradbury
Barbarians of Mars (1965) a.k.a. *Masters of the Pit* (1971); as Edward P. Bradbury
The Twilight Man (1965) a.k.a. *The Shores of Death* (1970)
The LSD Dossier (1966); as Roger Harris
Somewhere in the Night (1966) revised as *The Chinese Agent* (1970); as Bill Barclay
Printer's Devil (1966) revised as *The Russian Intelligence* (1980); as Bill Barclay
The Jewel in the Skull (1967); revised (1977)
The Wrecks of Time (1967) (U.S.), censored; a.k.a. *The Rituals of Infinity* (1971) (UK), uncensored
The Mad God's Amulet (1969) a.k.a. *Sorcerer's Amulet* (1968) (U.S. title); revised (1977)

The Sword of the Dawn (1969); revised (1977)
The Final Programme (1968); censored in U.S.; revised (1979)
The Runestaff (1969) a.k.a. *The Secret of the Runestaff* (1969) (U.S. title); revised (1977)
Behold the Man (1969)
The Black Corridor (1969); with Hilary Bailey (uncredited)
The Ice Schooner (1969); revised (1977), (1986)
The Eternal Champion (1970); revised (1977)
Phoenix in Obsidian (1970) a.k.a. *The Silver Warriors* (1973) (U.S. title)
A Cure For Cancer (1971); revised (1979)
The Knight of the Swords (1971)
The Queen of the Swords (1971)
The King of the Swords (1971)
The Warlord of the Air (1971) (U.S. title); a.k.a. *The War Lord of the Air* (1971); censored in UK, restored in *A Nomad of the Time Steams* (1993)
The Sleeping Sorceress (1971) a.k.a. *The Vanishing Tower* (1977)
Breakfast in the Ruins (1971)
The English Assassin (1972); revised (1979)
An Alien Heat (1972)
Elric of Melniboné (1972) a.k.a. *The Dreaming City* (1972) (U.S. title); with unauthorized edits
Count Brass (1973)
The Bull and the Spear (1973)
The Champion of Garathorm (1973)
The Oak and the Ram (1973)
The Sword and the Stallion (1974)
The Land Leviathan (1974)
The Hollow Lands (1974)
The Quest for Tanelorn (1975)
The Distant Suns (1975); as Philip James with James Cawthorn
The Sailor on the Seas of Fate (1976)
The End of All Songs (1976)
The Adventures of Una Persson and Catherine Cornelius in the Twentieth Century (1976)

The Transformation of Miss Mavis Ming (1977) a.k.a. *A Messiah at the End of Time* (1977) (U.S. title); revised as *Constant Fire* (1993)
The Condition of Muzak (1977)
Gloriana (1978); revised (1993)
The Golden Barge (1979); written 1958
The Great Rock 'n' Roll Swindle (1980)
Byzantium Endures (1981); censored in U.S.
The Entropy Tango (1981)
The War Hound and the World's Pain (1981)
The Steel Tsar (1981); substantially revised in *A Nomad of the Time Streams* (1993)
The Brothel in Rosenstrasse (1982)
The Laughter of Carthage (1984)
The Dragon in the Sword (1986)
The City in the Autumn Stars (1986)
Mother London (1988)
The Fortress of the Pearl (1989)
The Revenge of the Rose (1991)
Jerusalem Commands (1992)
Blood (1995)
The War Amongst the Angels (1996)
King of the City (2000)
Silverheart (2000); with Storm Constantine
The Dreamthief's Daughter (2001)
The Skrayling Tree (2003)
The White Wolf's Son (2005)
The Vengeance of Rome (2006)
Doctor Who: The Coming of the Terraphiles (2010)

COLLECTIONS & ANTHOLOGIES

The Stealer of Souls (1963)
The Deep Fix (1966); as James Colvin
The Time Dweller (1969)

The Singing Citadel (1970)
The Nature of the Catastrophe (1971); anthology, stories by Moorcock and others
Legends from the End of Time (1976)
Moorcock's Book of Martyrs (1976) a.k.a. *Dying For Tomorrow* (1976) (U.S. title)
The Lives and Times of Jerry Cornelius (1976); revised (1987), (2003)
Sojan (1977)
The Weird of the White Wolf (1977); formerly *The Singing Citadel/The Stealer of Souls*
The Bane of the Black Sword (1977); formerly *The Stealer of Souls/The Singing Citadel*
My Experiences in the Third World War (1980)
Elric at the End of Time (1984)
The Opium General and Other Stories (1984)
Casablanca (1989)
The New Nature of the Catastrophe (1993); anthology, stories by Moorcock and others (revised from 1971)
Fabulous Harbours (1995) a.k.a. *Fabulous Harbors* (1995) (U.S. title)
Lunching with the Antichrist (1995)
Tales from the Texas Woods (1997)
London Bone (2001)
The Metatemporal Detective (2007)
Elric: The Stealer of Souls (2008)
Elric: To Rescue Tanelorn (2008)
Elric: The Sleeping Sorceress (2008)
Elric: Duke Elric (2009)
The Best of Michael Moorcock (2009)
Elric: In the Dream Realms (2009)
Elric: Swords and Roses (2010)
Modem Times 2.0 (2011)

DIGESTS, PAMPHLETS, AND NOVELLAS

Caribbean Crisis (1962); digest, as Desmond Reid with James Cawthorn (text rewritten by publisher)

The Jade Man's Eyes (1973); novella, revised in *The Sailor on the Seas of Fate* (1976)

Epic Pooh (1978); pamphlet, nonfiction, reprinted in *Wizardry and Wild Romance* (1987)

The Real Life Mr. Newman (1979); pamphlet, originally published in *The Deep Fix* (1966)

The Retreat from Liberty (1983); pamphlet, non-fiction

Elric at the End of Time (1987); illustrated novella, with Rodney Matthews

The Birds of the Moon (1995); pamphlet, reprinted in *Fabulous Harbours* (1995)

Behold the Man: The Thirtieth Anniversary Edition (1996); novella, originally published in *New Worlds #166* (1966)

Firing the Cathedral (2002); novella, reprinted in *The Lives and Times of Jerry Cornelius* (2003)

The Mystery of the Texas Twister (2004); novella, published with *Argosy #1*, reprinted in *The Metatemporal Detective* (2007)

NONFICTION BOOKS

Letters from Hollywood (1986)

Wizardry and Wild Romance (1987); revised (2004)

Fantasy - The 100 Best Books (1988); with James Cawthorn

Death Is No Obstacle (1992); with Colin Greenland

Into the Media Web (2010); selected nonfiction, 1956–2006

London Peculiar and Other Nonfiction (2012)

GRAPHIC STORIES AND ILLUSTRATED BOOKS

The Adventures of Jerry Cornelius: The English Assassin (1969–70); with M. John Harrison, Mal Dean, and Richard Glyn Jones, in *International Times #57–71*

"A Sword Called Stormbringer" (1972); with James Cawthorn, Roy Thomas, and Barry Windsor Smith, in *Conan the Barbarian #14*

"The Green Empress of Melniboné" (1972); with James Cawthorn, Roy Thomas and Barry Windsor Smith, in *Conan the Barbarian #15*

Elric: The Return to Melniboné (1973); with Philippe Druillet

The Swords of Heaven, the Flowers of Hell (1979); with Howard Chaykin

Michael Moorcock's Multiverse (1999); with Walter Simonson, Mark Reeves, and John Ridgeway

"Blitz Kid" (2002); with Walter Simonson, in *9-11: The World's Finest Comic Book Writers and Artists Tell Stories To Remember, Volume 2*

"The Black Blade of the Barbary Coast" (2005), with Jerry Ordway, in *Tom Strong #31–32*

Elric: The Making of a Sorcerer (2006); with Walter Simonson

The Sunday Books (2010); words by Moorcock, pictures by Mervyn Peake (published in French)

SELECTED OMNIBUSES

Tales from the End of Time (1976) (U.S. omnibus)

The Elric Saga, Part I (1977) (U.S. omnibus)

The Elric Saga, Part II (1977) (U.S. omnibus)

The Cornelius Chronicles (1977) (U.S. omnibus) as two volumes in the UK: *The Cornelius Chronicles Book One & The Cornelius Chronicles Book Two* (1987) a.k.a. *The Cornelius Quartet* (1993)

The Swords Trilogy (1977) (U.S. title) a.k.a. *The Swords of Corum*

(1986) (UK title) a.k.a. *Corum* (1992) (UK title) a.k.a. *Corum: The Coming of Chaos (*1997) (U.S. title) a.k.a. *Corum: The Prince in the Scarlet Robe* (2002) (UK title)

The Chronicles of Corum (1978) a.k.a. *The Prince with the Silver Hand* (1993) a.k.a. *Corum: The Prince with the Silver Hand* (1999) (U.S. title)

The History of the Runestaff (1979) (UK omnibus) a.k.a. *Hawkmoon*; revised (1993)

The Dancers at the End of Time (1981)

Warrior of Mars (1981) (UK title) a.k.a. *Kane of Old Mars* (1998) (U.S. title)

The Nomad of Time (1982) a.k.a. *A Nomad of the Time Streams*; revised (1993)

The Chronicles of Castle Brass (1985) (UK omnibus) a.k.a. *Count Brass*; revised (1993)

The Cornelius Chronicles, Vol. II (1986) (U.S. omnibus)

The Cornelius Chronicles, Vol. III (1987) (U.S. omnibus)

Von Bek (1992)

The Eternal Champion (1992)

Sailing to Utopia (1993)

Elric of Melniboné (1993) (UK title) a.k.a. *Elric: Song of the Black Sword* (1995) (U.S. title)

Legends from the End of Time (1993)

Stormbringer (1993) (UK title) a.k.a. *Elric: The Stealer of Souls* (1998) (U.S. title)

Earl Aubec (1993) (UK title) a.k.a. *Earl Aubec and Other Stories* (1999) (U.S. title)

A Cornelius Calendar (1993) (UK omnibus)

Behold the Man and Other Stories (1994) (UK omnibus)

The Roads Between the Worlds (1996) (U.S. omnibus)

Elric (2001)

The Elric Saga, Part III (2002) (U.S. omnibus)

Jerry Cornell's Comic Capers (2005)

The Elric Saga, Part IV (2005) (U.S. omnibus)

EDITED ANTHOLOGIES

The Best of New Worlds (1965)
Best SF Stories from New Worlds (1967)
Best Stories from New Worlds II (1968)
Best SF Stories from New Worlds 3 (1968)
The Traps of Time (1968)
Best SF Stories from New Worlds 4 (1969)
Best SF Stories from New Worlds 5 (1969)
The Inner Landscape (1969) (uncredited)
Best SF Stories from New Worlds 6 (1970)
Best SF Stories from New Worlds 7 (1971)
Best SF Stories from New Worlds 8 (1974)
Before Armageddon (1975)
England Invaded (1977)
New Worlds: An Anthology (1983, revised 2004)

ABOUT THE AUTHOR

Born in London and raised on Mars (or so he claims), Michael Moorcock is perhaps the single most important figure in modern science fiction, and the most unlikely to get an O.B.E. The author of over seventy novels and countless stories, essays, rock songs, comics, delicious screeds, and dangerous rants, he lives in rural Texas and Paris, France. And in Legend as well.

"I admire a man who can look cool on a camel."
—Bessy Burroughs, *Modem Times 2.0*

PM PRESS OUTSPOKEN AUTHORS

The Left Left Behind
Terry Bisson
978-1-60486-086-3
$12

Hugo and Nebula award-winner Terry Bisson is best known for his short stories, which range from the southern sweetness of "Bears Discover Fire" to the alienated aliens of "They're Made out of Meat." He is also a 1960s New Left vet with a history of activism and an intact (if battered) radical ideology.

The *Left Behind* novels (about the so-called "Rapture" in which all the born-agains ascend straight to heaven) are among the bestselling Christian books in the U.S., describing in lurid detail the adventures of those "left behind" to battle the Anti-Christ. Put Bisson and the Born-Agains together, and what do you get? *The Left Left Behind*—a sardonic, merciless, tasteless, take-no-prisoners satire of the entire apocalyptic enterprise that spares no one-predatory preachers, goth lingerie, Pacifica radio, Indian casinos, gangsta rap, and even "art cars" at Burning Man.

Plus: "Special Relativity," a one-act drama that answers the question: When Albert Einstein, Paul Robeson, J. Edgar Hoover are raised from the dead at an anti-Bush rally, which one wears the dress? As with all Outspoken Author books, there is a deep interview and autobiography: at length, in-depth, no-holds-barred, and all-bets-off: an extended tour though the mind and work, the history and politics of our Outspoken Author. Surprises are promised.

PM PRESS OUTSPOKEN AUTHORS

The Lucky Strike
Kim Stanley Robinson
978-1-60486-085-6
$12

Combining dazzling speculation with a profoundly humanist vision, Kim Stanley Robinson is known as not only the most literary but also the most progressive (read "radical") of today's top-rank SF authors. His bestselling Mars Trilogy tells the epic story of the future colonization of the red planet, and the revolution that inevitably follows. His latest novel, *Galileo's Dream*, is a stunning combination of historical drama and far-flung space opera, in which the ten dimensions of the universe itself are rewoven to ensnare history's most notorious torturers.

The Lucky Strike, the classic and controversial story Robinson has chosen for PM's new Outspoken Authors series, begins on a lonely Pacific island, where a crew of untested men are about to take off in an untried aircraft with a deadly payload that will change our world forever. Until something goes wonderfully wrong.

Plus: *A Sensitive Dependence on Initial Conditions*, in which Robinson dramatically deconstructs "alternate history" to explore what might have been if things had gone differently over Hiroshima that day.

As with all Outspoken Author books, there is a deep interview and autobiography: at length, in-depth, no-holds-barred and all-bets-off: an extended tour though the mind and work, the history and politics of our Outspoken Author. Surprises are promised.

PM PRESS OUTSPOKEN AUTHORS

Mammoths of the Great Plains
Eleanor Arnason
978-1-60486-075-7
$12

When President Thomas Jefferson sent Lewis and Clark to explore the West, he told them to look especially for mammoths. Jefferson had seen bones and tusks of the great beasts in Virginia, and he suspected—he hoped!—that they might still roam the Great Plains. In Eleanor Arnason's imaginative alternate history, they do: shaggy herds thunder over the grasslands, living symbols of the oncoming struggle between the Native peoples and the European invaders. And in an unforgettable saga that soars from the badlands of the Dakotas to the icy wastes of Siberia, from the Russian Revolution to the AIM protests of the 1960s, Arnason tells of a modern woman's struggle to use the weapons of DNA science to fulfill the ancient promises of her Lakota heritage.

PLUS: "Writing SF During World War III," and an Outspoken Interview that takes you straight into the heart and mind of one of today's edgiest and most uncompromising speculative authors.

Praise:
"Eleanor Arnason nudges both human and natural history around so gently in this tale that you hardly know you're not in the world-as-we-know-it until you're quite at home in a North Dakota where you've never been before, listening to your grandmother tell you the world." —Ursula K. Le Guin

FRIENDS OF

These are indisputably momentous times—the financial system is melting down globally and the Empire is stumbling. Now more than ever there is a vital need for radical ideas.

In the three years since its founding—and on a mere shoestring—PM Press has risen to the formidable challenge of publishing and distributing knowledge and entertainment for the struggles ahead. With over 100 releases to date, we have published an impressive and stimulating array of literature, art, music, politics, and culture. Using every available medium, we've succeeded in connecting those hungry for ideas and information to those putting them into practice.

Friends of PM allows you to directly help impact, amplify, and revitalize the discourse and actions of radical writers, filmmakers, and artists. It provides us with a stable foundation from which we can build upon our early successes and provides a much-needed subsidy for the materials that can't necessarily pay their own way. You can help make that happen – and receive every new title automatically delivered to your door once a month – by joining as a Friend of PM Press. And, we'll throw in a free T-Shirt when you sign up.

Here are your options:

- $25 a month: Get all books and pamphlets plus 50% discount on all webstore purchases.
- $25 a month: Get all CDs and DVDs plus 50% discount on all webstore purchases.
- $40 a month: Get all PM Press releases plus 50% discount on all webstore purchases
- $100 a month: Sustainer. - Everything plus PM merchandise, free downloads, and 50% discount on all webstore purchases.

For those who can't afford $25 or more a month, we're introducing Sustainer Rates at $15, $10 and $5. Sustainers get a free PM Press t-shirt and a 50% discount on all purchases from our website.

Just go to **WWW.PMPRESS.ORG** to sign up. Your Visa or Mastercard will be billed once a month, until you tell us to stop. Or until our efforts succeed in bringing the revolution around. Or the financial meltdown of Capital makes plastic redundant. Whichever comes first.

PM Press was founded at the end of 2007 by a small collection of folks with decades of publishing, media, and organizing experience. PM Press co-conspirators have published and distributed hundreds of books, pamphlets, CDs, and DVDs. Members of PM have founded enduring book fairs, spearheaded victorious tenant organizing campaigns, and worked closely with bookstores, academic conferences, and even rock bands to deliver political and challenging ideas to all walks of life. We're old enough to know what we're doing and young enough to know what's at stake.

We seek to create radical and stimulating fiction and non-fiction books, pamphlets, t-shirts, visual and audio materials to entertain, educate and inspire you. We aim to distribute these through every available channel with every available technology—whether that means you are seeing anarchist classics at our bookfair stalls; reading our latest vegan cookbook at the café; downloading geeky fiction e-books; or digging new music and timely videos from our website.

PM Press is always on the lookout for talented and skilled volunteers, artists, activists and writers to work with. If you have a great idea for a project or can contribute in some way, please get in touch.

PM Press
PO Box 23912
Oakland CA 94623
510-658-3906
www.pmpress.org